Eva pushed herself  **straightened her fit**

Their eyes met. She raised her hand, waving feebly.

The bright smile on Clark's handsome face fell. His rich brown complexion turned a pale shade of gray. His eyelids lowered, as if he couldn't believe what he was seeing. In that moment, Eva wished she could teleport herself back to Black Willow.

"Dr. Malone," Brandi began. "I'd like for you to meet—"

"Dr. Eva Gordon," Clark interjected, his low tone tinged with a slight tremor.

"Hello, Dr. Malone," she practically choked through quivering lips.

Brandi's head swiveled from side to side. "Wait, you two know each other?"

"We do," Eva murmured, her gaze fixated on Clark's pulsating temples. It was a trait she remembered him exhibiting whenever a stressful situation presented itself. "Dr. Malone and I attended Cedar Rapids Medical School together."

Dear Reader,

Do you believe in second chances? This trope is one of my favorites to write, and I truly enjoyed exploring the possibility of Clark and Eva finding their happily-ever-after the second time around in *ER Doc's Las Vegas Reunion*.

My hero and heroine have a strong foundation as they were close friends during medical school. But once that bond was broken, neither of them thought they'd find their way back to one another. Then fate intervenes, and Clark and Eva are forced to work together under strained circumstances, all while fighting their undeniable chemistry. Their rocky past leaves them both afraid to explore something more. But as feelings resurface, truth bombs are dropped and emotions come to a head, forcing them to revisit mistakes once made in order to determine where they should go from here.

Clark and Eva's story is a reminder that true love, no matter how complicated, always prevails. This novel was such a joy to write. I hope you enjoy reading these characters' journey to happiness!

XOXO,

Denise

ER DOC'S LAS VEGAS REUNION

DENISE N. WHEATLEY

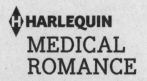
HARLEQUIN

MEDICAL ROMANCE

HARLEQUIN®
MEDICAL
ROMANCE™

Recycling programs
for this product may
not exist in your area.

ISBN-13: 978-1-335-59527-0

ER Doc's Las Vegas Reunion

Copyright © 2024 by Denise N. Wheatley

Harlequin Enterprises ULC
22 Adelaide St. West, 41st Floor
Toronto, Ontario M5H 4E3, Canada
www.Harlequin.com

Printed in U.S.A.

Denise N. Wheatley loves happy endings and the art of storytelling. Her novels run the romance gamut, and she strives to pen entertaining books that embody matters of the heart. She's an RWA member and holds a BA in English from the University of Illinois. When Denise isn't writing, she enjoys watching true-crime TV and chatting with readers. Follow her on social media.

Instagram: @Denise_Wheatley_Writer
Twitter: @DeniseWheatley
BookBub: @DeniseNWheatley
Goodreads: Denise N. Wheatley

ER Doc's Las Vegas Reunion
is Denise N. Wheatley's debut book for
Harlequin Medical Romance.

Also by Denise N. Wheatley

Harlequin Intrigue

A West Coast Crime Story

The Heart-Shaped Murders
Danger in the Nevada Desert
Homicide at Vincent Vineyard

An Unsolved Mystery Book

Cold Case True Crime

Bayou Christmas Disappearance
Backcountry Cover-Up

Visit the Author Profile page at Harlequin.com.

To my mother, Donna, who is the reason for it all.

**Praise for
Denise N. Wheatley**

"I absolutely loved this book by Denise… A well written, fast paced story guaranteed to have you on the edge of your seat. I definitely recommend this one."

—*Goodreads* on *Bayou Christmas Disappearance*

PROLOGUE

EVA'S CELL PHONE vibrated through her black satin clutch. She quickly pulled it out, expecting to see her fiancé's name flash across the screen. But it was Amanda, her friend and fellow ER doctor at the Black Willow Medical Clinic, calling for the third time.

"Hey," Eva whispered into the phone. "I can't talk now. I'm about to—"

"Let me guess. Attend yet another elaborate campaign event with your devastatingly handsome, soon-to-be senator fiancé?"

"No, not tonight. Kyle and I are actually having a quiet dinner at the Chateau Eilean."

"Ooh, the hottest new restaurant in all of Iowa? Fancy. Just the two of you?"

"Yes, can you believe it? No campaign manager and no entourage. Which is nice considering we haven't had a date night in months."

Eva stopped in front of a gold antique mirror inside the chateau's lobby and smoothed her long loose waves, then tightened the belt on her red wrap dress. She didn't know whether it was the triweekly spin classes or wedding planning stress that had whittled her size 8 frame down to a 6. Either way, her charmeuse trumpet bridal gown had to be taken in a few extra inches after the last fitting.

"I wish tonight could be all about rekindling the romance that's taken a back seat to our busy schedules," Eva continued. "But I've got to use this rare time alone with Kyle to finalize plans for the big day." She paused, wincing at the death stare on the hostess's face. "Listen, I've gotta go. Phones aren't allowed in here and I'm pushing it. I'll call you later."

She glanced at her watch, realizing she was fifteen minutes late.

Good. Let Kyle wait on me for once…

A Little Leaguer had shown up to the clinic at the last minute with a hamate hook fracture that Eva had to cast before heading to dinner, which set her back. But while she worked hard to stick to her schedule and be on time whenever possible, it was Kyle who always ran late these days thanks to his unpredictable campaign activities.

"Hello," Eva said to the hostess, whose scowl quickly transformed into an artificially sweetened smile. "My name is Eva Gordon. I'm meeting Kyle Benson for dinner. The reservation should be in his name."

"Yes, Dr. Gordon. Right this way."

The haughty, model-thin greeter led Eva through the elaborate Victorian-style dining room to a table near the window. It was empty. No Kyle.

Late. Per usual.

A server approached the moment she sat down.

"Good evening, Dr. Gordon. May I offer you a beverage while you wait for Mr. Benson? A glass of wine, perhaps?"

"A glass of cabernet sauvignon would be perfect. Thank you."

She checked her phone. It was almost seven twenty. Their reservation was at seven. Kyle hadn't called, nor had he texted.

Eva sent him a message asking what time he'd be there, then glanced around the beautiful eatery. Crystal chandeliers hung from the vaulted ceiling. Intricate carvings outlined the cream wooden walls, which were adorned with vintage oil paintings. Blue silk chairs matched the curtains hanging from arched bay windows.

The chateau was buzzing with the who's who of Black Willow. Bankers, attorneys and politicians hobnobbed over charcuterie boards, steaks, seafood and pasta. Eva's mouth watered at the sight. She hadn't eaten since breakfast.

Just as she checked the phone once again, a commotion erupted near the entrance.

Eva watched as Kyle came strolling through the restaurant, stopping at practically every table on the way to theirs.

The handsome six-foot-three former soccer player turned political pundit was hard to miss. His movie-star smile could light up a night sky. His almond-shaped brown eyes danced when he spoke on his plans to change the world. His warm demeanor made people feel as though they were all that mattered.

The chateau's manager rushed over and shook Kyle's hand. "It's great to see you here tonight, Mr. Benson. So, what do you think? Is this the best night of the week to come out and rub elbows with Black Willow's elite or what?"

"It certainly is. I've already got my eye on several potential donors."

Eva dug her fingernails into the linen tablecloth.

So that's why we're here. To network. Not spend a quiet evening alone.

"Good luck with that," the manager told Kyle. "If there's anything I can do for you, please do not hesitate to let me know."

"Will do, Douglas. Thank you."

Kyle glanced over at Eva, grinning and waving as if he were about to deliver a victory speech.

"Hey, babe," he breathed, finally reaching their table. "Sorry I'm late."

She arched her neck for a kiss, despite being slightly irritated. Kyle's lips barely grazed her cheek before he greeted a group of men seated nearby, then searched for the server.

Let it go. Don't start the night off on a sour note.

"I was going to order appetizers," Eva said, "but couldn't decide on what to get. Everything looks so good."

"Well, I'm glad you didn't. I can't stay long. I've got to get back to the office soon. Things are really heating up."

"Wait, what about dinner?"

"Can't do it. I've only got about thirty minutes to spare, if that. Just enough time to have a quick drink."

Eva tossed her menu to the side. "What's so important that you're skipping out on what I thought was a special date night for just the two of us?"

"A meeting with my campaign manager. Stan added a last-minute speech to my calendar that I need to prepare for. It's happening first thing tomorrow morning down at the mayor's office. This is a big deal for me, Eva. And great exposure. Several media outlets will be there. I've got to be ready."

She opened her mouth to speak but was interrupted when the server approached with her wine. While Kyle ordered a whiskey sour, Eva pulled out a stack of floral design photos.

"Since you have to leave so soon, can we at least look through the arrangements that Louise pulled together for the wedding?" She slid a picture in front of him. "I love this one. The etched crystal vase is gorgeous. And the various shades of pink peonies with eucalyptus added throughout is just perfection. But I also love the idea of keeping things traditional and going with roses. Or maybe even calla lilies. What do you think?"

Kyle remained silent, too busy typing away on his phone to respond.

"*Excuse* me," Eva said stiffly. "Could I at least get my allotted thirty minutes to finalize these plans before you have to leave? We're going to end up with a flowerless ceremony if we don't make a decision and place the order—"

He held up a finger. "One second. I need to approve a couple of key points that Stan thinks I should add to my speech."

Eva dropped the stack of photos and gulped down several sips of wine. Shards of anger sliced at her chest while her heartbeat pounded inside her eardrums. She was *this close* to suggesting they nix the wedding ceremony altogether and exchange vows at the courthouse once the election was finally over.

Kyle didn't set his phone aside until the server brought over his drink. He took a long swallow, then rubbed his hands together.

"You know, I think I might go off script a little bit during my speech. Throw in a couple of bullet points on my education initiatives. I could cover how parents should be receiving school curricula, and suggest that fundraisers be held throughout the year in support of various scholarship programs. What do you think?"

Eva slowly exhaled. "I think those are both good ideas, Kyle. But can we just take a few minutes to look over the floral arrangements and choose the ones we want—"

His cell phone buzzed. He grabbed it, then began typing away once again.

"Kyle!" Eva said, louder than she'd intended.

He jumped in his seat. Several patrons turned and stared.

Kyle glanced at the nearby tables, smiling sheepishly before throwing Eva a look. "Will you please keep your voice down?"

"Sorry. I just wish you would tear yourself away from that phone and listen to me for once. Your *fiancée.* I understand that you've got work to do, but so do I. I left the clinic early tonight to be here with you. You're already cutting our evening short. The least you could do is help me with all this planning. I've done most of it on my own. A little input would be nice."

He dropped his head in his hand. The server approached and asked if they were ready to order. Kyle shooed him away.

Eva sat there silently, waiting for him to apologize and look through the floral designs.

"I can't do this," he muttered instead.

She reached over and caressed his arm. "Come on, Kyle. Of course you can do this. I've narrowed the choices down to four. All you have to do is pick one. As for your speech, you'll knock it out of the park, just like you always do."

"I'm not talking about flower arrangements, Eva," he snapped, pulling away from her. "Or my speech. I'm talking about us. I can't do *us* anymore."

She stared across the table through wide eyes, certain she'd misheard him.

"I—I'm sorry," Kyle continued, his voice barely a whisper. "But this is…this is too much. There's no way I can run a successful campaign, win the election *and* marry you. So I think we should call off the wedding."

Everything around Eva blurred, except for his sullen expression. She sat silently, waiting for him to recant the statement. But he didn't. He just continued sipping his drink while avoiding her stunned gaze.

"Hold on," she uttered, her voice trembling with shock. "Let me get this straight. You're telling me that you want to cancel our wedding because of an election that you're already on track to win?"

"Can you lower your voice? People are looking at us."

"*Kyle*, you just ended our relationship, and you're worried about who's looking at us? Oh, but wait. Why am I surprised? You've always been overly obsessed with your image. That's all that matters to you. To hell with reality. As long as you're keeping up appearances, you're good."

"Okay," he said, pushing away from the table. "I'm going to end this conversation now before things get ugly."

"Oh, trust me. Things can't get any uglier than they already are. Thank you, Kyle."

"Thank me? For what?"

"For wasting the last five years of my life!" she snapped before jumping up and storming out of the restaurant.

Anger coursed through Eva's chest as she ran to her car. But underneath it was the pain and confusion of knowing such a huge part of her life was over, and that for the first time ever, she had no clue what her future would hold.

Eva paced back and forth across the dark hardwood floor of her chic two-bedroom loft. She stopped at her desk, plopped down in the chair and logged in to her online journal. While waiting for it to open, an ad popped up.

"Weird," she mumbled, double-checking to make sure her pop-up blocker was on. It was.

The words *Are You Looking for a Change?* flashed across the screen in bold red letters.

"Hell, yeah, I'm looking for a change."

Eva clicked on the ad and leaned in closer, her eyes squinting as she read the details.

Hello! Do you work in the medical field? If so, are you interested in making a change? If the answer is yes, then we have an exciting opportunity for you! Las Vegas's Fremont General Hospital is looking to fill temporary positions in our neonatal, radiation, intensive care and emergency room departments.

"A temp job in the ER?" she murmured, double-clicking the emergency room button. It opened a new screen.

Fremont General Hospital's state-of-the-art ER is an intense, fast-paced environment, where the responsibility is as great as the reward. We are searching for an experienced emergency room doctor with in-depth knowledge of current medical treatments and procedures. Keen attention to detail along with excellent analytical and communication skills are a must. If you thrive on fascinating, fulfilling experiences, and possess the ability to think and act quickly, then click the link below to apply!

Eva's fingertips hovered over the keyboard. She thought about the moment Kyle spoke the words *I can't do us anymore.* Imagined all the scrutiny she'd be under once their small, gossipy town got word that their wedding, which had been dubbed "the event of the decade", had been canceled. The struggle to mend her broken heart, along with the humiliation, would be unbearable.

She'd always done the right thing. Followed in her father's footsteps by becoming a top doctor in her field and withstanding the pressure to be the best, just as he had. Abided by her mother's fervent desire for her to marry well by getting together with Kyle soon after he'd been crowned Black Willow's most eligible bachelor, then accepting his proposal. That had all worked for Eva, at least for a while.

When she and Kyle had met at a charity event five years ago, Eva felt as though he could be the man for her. His charm, his charisma, the way he seemingly adored her…it didn't take long for Eva to fall in love. But as Kyle's political career began to blossom, their relationship withered. His focus was solely on work as each new achievement grabbed his attention, making him crave more of the professional spotlight and less of time spent with her. Eva had thought his proposal would bring about a fresh start for them both. When nothing changed, she wondered whether Kyle really wanted the marriage, or simply the look of having a successful ER doctor on his arm.

Playing it safe to appease others had gotten

her nowhere. Now it was Eva's turn to do things her way.

"Here goes nothing," she said grimly before clicking the link and filling out the application.

CHAPTER ONE

Month one

"HERE WE ARE, Dr. Gordon."

Eva's heart dropped to the soles of her feet. She stared out the Tesla's back-seat window, eyeing Fremont General Hospital's sleek reflective glass and white cement exterior.

The crowded driveway was bustling with activity. Cars and emergency vehicles maneuvered their way around a beautiful garden filled with exotic succulents. A steady stream of guests, patients and hospital workers flowed in and out of the automatic glass doors. It was a far cry from the simpler inner workings of her clinic back home.

Eva, you're not in Black Willow anymore...

The driver's phone dinged, indicating another pickup request. He turned in his seat and cleared his throat. "Best of luck to you, Doctor."

"Oh, umm...sorry. I should let you be on your way. Thank you."

Her calf muscles trembled as she stepped out of the car. Eva's first day on the job, in a big new city no less, had sent her entire nervous system into a buzzing frenzy.

What in the world have I gotten myself into?

The last two weeks had been a whirlwind. Despite spontaneously applying for Fremont General's temporary ER position, Eva had struggled to recover from her breakup. She'd avoided all social functions and buried herself in work, while constantly refreshing her email inbox in hopes of hearing from Fremont's hospital administrator.

It took five days to find out that her application had been accepted and she'd landed the job. Since then, she'd had to console her supervisor, who was completely distraught upon hearing that Eva was taking a leave of absence, hire a house sitter, bid adieu to her family and friends, then jet off to Las Vegas, all without telling her ex-fiancé that she was leaving.

"And now, here I am," she whispered to herself. "Here we go."

Eva took a deep breath and walked inside the hospital's bright, airy lobby. Beams of light shone through the woven timber ceilings, highlighting vivid floral murals covering the walls. Plush leather chairs lined the vast waiting area. The space felt more like a lavish hotel than a hospital.

I could get used to this, she thought, making her way to the reception desk.

"Good morning," the receptionist said. "May I help you?"

"Yes, my name is Dr. Eva Gordon. I'm scheduled to meet Nurse Brandi Bennett here at the front desk. She works in the emergency room—"

"Dr. Gordon?" a petite, curly-haired blonde with rosy cheeks and a warm smile asked as she bounced toward Eva. "Hello there. I'm Nurse Bennett. But please, call me Brandi."

Eva shook her extended hand. "Hello, Brandi. It's nice to meet you. And finally put a face to the emails. Thanks again for all the advice you shared before my move here. It made things so much easier."

"You're welcome. I was happy to help. Trust me, I know what it's like to leave your small town behind on a whim and move to a big city. I'm here by way of Clemmington, California, which is only a few hours away. Your commute from Black Willow, Iowa, was a much longer one."

"It was," Eva replied, glancing around the lobby. "I just hope I can adjust quickly."

"I'm sure you will. This is going to be an amazing experience. It certainly has been for me. Are you ready to take a tour of the facility?"

The knots in Eva's stomach slowly unraveled, transforming into sprouts of excitement. "Yes, I'm ready."

"Great. We'll start on the top floor, where the

coronary and intensive care units are located, then work our way down. I'll save the emergency room for last. Follow me."

As the women headed toward the elevator, Brandi turned to Eva. "So, what was it about the temporary position here at Fremont General that pulled you away from home, if I may ask?"

"It's a long story. But for now, let's just say that a change of scenery was much needed."

"So, that's it in a nutshell," Brandi said. "A rather large nutshell, but you get the gist."

"I do," Eva told her. "It's a lot to take in. This is such a beautiful hospital. I'm sure I'll get lost more times than I can count. Hopefully it won't take long to learn my way around." She glanced up ahead. "And now, saving the best for last?"

"Yes, the emergency room. We're almost there. The cafeteria is on the way. Would you like to stop in and grab a cup of coffee?"

"That would be wonderful. I can't believe I've lasted this long without my daily caffeine fix."

Eva followed Brandi inside the sunny dining hall. They passed an array of food stations, from sushi and hot dog stands to pasta and salad bars. Right before they approached the Drip & Sip Coffee Stop, a familiar figure appeared near the delicatessen.

"*Wait*, is that…?" Eva began, thinking she might have just spotted Idris Elba.

No, it couldn't be. There aren't any cameras around filming a movie. So why would he be here wearing a lab coat?

"Is that who?" Brandi asked, glancing around the area.

Eva hesitated, not wanting to admit that she'd mistaken a doctor for a movie star. "Oh, it's nothing. So what do you recommend?"

"My go-to is the iced shaken espresso with a shot of oat milk and a dash of stevia. It keeps me on my toes throughout the day."

"Sounds like that's exactly what I need."

"Awesome. I'll grab a couple."

While Brandi placed their order, Eva's eyes drifted toward the exit. The Idris Elba look-alike was walking out. Despite his back being to her, Eva couldn't help but feel as though she knew him. The way his tall, lean build broke into a swaggering gait, his short wavy hair tapered down the back of his neck, and his large hands gestured emphatically all rang familiar bells.

"Here you go," Brandi said, handing Eva a cup. "I hope you like it."

"I'm sure I will." She took a long sip, closing her eyes as the rich, smoky java settled into her taste buds. "Mmm, this is delicious. Great choice."

"Awesome. Ready to head to the ER?"

"Absolutely."

A burst of exhilaration shot through Eva's

veins as her nude pumps clicked along the speck-led white tile.

Finally, a look at my new digs for the next three months...

The pair exited the cafeteria and made a left turn.

"Oh, hold on," Brandi said, staring down the other end of the hallway. "Dr. Malone!" she called out.

Eva followed her gaze. It fell on the Idris doppelgänger. His head was buried in a file. A husky, bald-headed man he was speaking with nudged him, then pointed at Brandi. He looked up, peering down the corridor.

"Do you have a minute?" Brandi asked. "I'd like for you to meet someone."

As the men walked toward them, Eva's entire body went numb.

"No..." she whispered. "It can't be..."

"I'm sorry?" Brandy asked her.

"That's—that's Dr. *who*?"

"Dr. Malone. Dr. Clark Malone, to be exact. He's one of our emergency room physicians, so you two will be working very closely together."

Eva's knees gave way. She leaned against the wall, her racing heart palpitating inside her throat as she struggled to grasp Brandi's words.

Clark Malone...

He and Eva shared a tumultuous past that she'd buried deep in the corners of her mind. Up until now. Because as he approached, a whirlwind of memories came racing to the forefront, the first being that he was no longer a handsome yet wiry young medical student. Clark had matured into a full-blown, broad-shouldered, extremely fine-looking man.

They'd met during their first year of medical school. Despite the undeniable chemistry between them, Eva and Clark had formed a tight platonic bond. Together they'd helped each other adjust to a new city, an extremely challenging course load and a rigorous schedule. While free time was sparse, they'd sneak off on occasion to Cedar Rapids, Iowa's Black Sheep Social Club for live jazz music, or Pub 217 for veggie black bean burgers. The friendship they'd built was solid, inimitable even. But all that had changed one night during their third year.

Hours of intense studying for a genetics exam, mixed with a few beers and joke-telling challenges, had turned an evening cramming session into a fiery romp between the sheets. While Clark had hoped that the moment would lead to much more, Eva had regretfully explained to him that she was laser-focused on her studies and couldn't continue anything that might jeopardize her medical goals.

She didn't, however, completely reject him. Eva had told Clark that while they couldn't be together back then, she was open to something more once they'd settled into their new jobs after graduation. In the meantime, they'd tried to remain friends, but things just weren't the same. They'd slowly drifted apart, then lost touch after graduation, with her staying in the Midwest while he'd jetted off to the West Coast.

Losing Clark as a friend had hurt her deeply. But Eva's aspirations had taken precedence over her emotions—she'd worked too hard to risk getting distracted. But she'd thought about him many times over the years—particularly that one steamy night they'd shared. While it had been amazing, Eva couldn't help but regret how it led to the demise of their friendship. She'd contemplated contacting Clark on numerous occasions but had always talked herself out of it. After the emotional roller-coaster ride they'd endured, she didn't think he would want to hear from her. Since he'd never reached out to her, either, Eva had figured he'd moved on and decided to do the same.

Now here he was, standing before her at Fremont General Hospital of all places.

What were the odds?

Eva pushed herself away from the wall and straightened her fitted black blazer. Their eyes met. She raised her hand, waving feebly.

The bright, welcoming smile on Clark's handsome face fell instantly as his jaws clenched. His rich brown complexion turned a pale shade of gray. His eyes narrowed, as if he couldn't believe what he was seeing. The reaction caused a hurt so deep that it left Eva wishing she could teleport herself straight back to Black Willow.

"Dr. Malone," Brandi began. "I'd like for you to meet—"

"Dr. Eva Gordon," Clark interjected coolly.

"Hello, Dr. Malone," she practically choked through quivering lips.

Brandi's head swiveled from side to side. "Wait, you two know each other?"

"We do," Eva murmured, her gaze fixated on Clark's pulsating temples. It was a trait she remembered him exhibiting whenever a stressful situation presented itself. "Dr. Malone and I attended Cedar Rapids Medical School together."

Clark squared his shoulders, folding his hands in front of him while staring at her.

His defense mechanism whenever he's guarding his feelings, Eva thought, surprised at how easy it was to read him after all these years.

"I…um…" Clark paused, his forehead creasing with confusion. "I'm surprised to see you here at Fremont General, Dr. Gordon. What brings you to Las Vegas?"

"Actually," Brandi chimed in, "Dr. Gordon has accepted a temporary assignment here in the ER for the next three months. So you two will be working very closely with each other, which should be an easy transition since you attended medical school together."

"Wait, you accepted *what*?" Clark barked right before his colleague stepped in and extended a hand.

"Dr. Gordon, welcome aboard. It's great to have you here."

"Oh!" Brandi uttered. "My apologies. I was so surprised to find out that Dr. Gordon and Dr. Malone know each other that I've forgotten my manners. Dr. Gordon, this is Leo Graham, our esteemed director of emergency medicine. Any questions or concerns you have, he's your go-to guy."

"It's nice to meet you, Director Graham."

"Likewise. And please, call me Leo."

Clark glanced down at his watch, then nudged Leo's shoulder. "We need to get back to your office. I've got some files to review with you, and several patients to check on. Dr. Gordon, welcome to Fremont General. I guess I'll be seeing you around."

"Great meeting you, Dr. Gor—" Leo began right before Clark grabbed his arm and dragged him in the opposite direction.

"We'll catch up with you two inside the ER!" Brandi called out to their backs. She turned to Eva. "Don't mind them. Things can get pretty hectic around here, so I'm sure they're just in a hurry. Are you ready to wrap up the tour?"

"Sure," Eva muttered, remorse burning her eyes as she watched Clark swiftly stride off.

He can't stand to even be in my presence. This isn't going to work. I shouldn't have come here.

"Wait," Eva continued hurriedly. "Before we finish the tour, I need to stop by the ladies' room. Is there one close by?"

"There is. It's straight ahead and to your right. Once you're done, why don't you meet me inside the emergency room? It'll be little farther down the hall on your left. Just follow the signs. You can't miss it."

"Thanks. I'll be right there."

Beads of perspiration popped up along Eva's hairline as she tore down the corridor. She dumped her coffee inside a trash receptacle, her stomach churning at the thought of ingesting anything.

This cannot be happening. This cannot be happening!

Just when she reached the restroom, a group of mothers with screaming toddlers in tow bolted inside. Eva continued down the hallway, her head spinning in search of a quiet nook.

Three empty phone booths appeared up ahead. Eva slipped inside the first one, pulled her cell phone from her purse and said, "Call Amanda Reinhart!" into the microphone.

Amanda picked up on the first ring. "Hey! How's it going out there in sunny Sin Cit—"

"*Amanda*! You will never, and I do mean *never*, guess who works at Fremont General."

"Wait, slow down. I can't understand you. I'll never guess *what*?"

"Who. Works. At. Fremont. General!"

"Who?"

"*Clark*. As in Clark Malone!"

Eva closed her eyes, sliding down the cool oakwood wall before plopping down onto a worn burgundy stool.

The other end of the phone went silent.

"Amanda? Are you still there?"

"I—I'm here. I just… I don't even know what to say, except *wow*. You and Clark, together again? You two didn't exactly leave medical school on the best of terms. So to be reunited with him after all these years, under these circumstances no less, is—"

"Wild as hell," Eva interjected.

"Exactly. And you all were such great friends. Until you slept together. You know, I never did understand why you didn't give him a chance after that. Especially considering how good the sex was, according to you."

"Amanda, please. You know why I didn't give him a chance back then. I was focused on graduating top of our class and landing my first-choice residency. I didn't have the time or the emotional bandwidth for a serious relationship."

"More like you were working to live up to

your father's legacy and appease your high-society mother—"

"Which is perfectly understandable considering everything they sacrificed for me, isn't it?" Eva interrupted. "Especially my mom. This is a generational thing. She watched her parents struggle for years, saving until they were in their mid-fifties to purchase their first house. Then my mother worked two jobs to help my father get through medical school. She didn't want to see me go through those same tribulations."

"Is that why she's always been so intent on you being with Kyle, too?"

"That is absolutely why. My mother loves that he comes from a good family and has done well for himself. She's old-school. She wants me to be well taken care of, despite me being able to take care of myself."

"And I understand all that, Eva. But this is *your* life. When are you going to start living it on your terms? You've proven to your parents that they did a wonderful job raising you. You are their wildest dream come true considering you've become such a successful doctor, just like your father. That's why everyone here at the clinic was so distraught when they found out you'd accepted this temporary assignment! Now, what about your dreams? Which I know include finding love again. I've always said that when it comes to Clark—"

"I know, I know," Eva interjected. "You've always said that I may have very well passed up the love of my life." A muscle pulled inside her chest at the sound of those words. "Right now, that's the last thing I need to hear. Can we please just focus on the issue at hand?"

"Sorry, my friend. I'm just being honest. But wait, what exactly is the issue at hand? You and Clark reuniting could be a good thing. Maybe this is the universe's way of bringing you two back together."

"Look, I just got dumped by my fiancé. The main reason I came to Las Vegas was to escape all the reminders of my heartbreak and heal in peace. I don't want to get caught up in another situation where I could get hurt again. Plus Clark seems to hate me. When we ran into each other just now, he couldn't wait to get away." Eva groaned loudly, slumping down deeper into the stool. "This was a mistake. I should come back home."

"You should do no such thing. Give this awesome opportunity a chance, Eva. And don't worry about Clark. He was probably just as shocked to see you as you were to see him. You two will find your footing, and hopefully even rekindle your old friendship. Trust me. There is more to this serendipitous reunion than you may think."

"I don't know about all that, but thanks for the

advice." Eva sighed, glancing at the time. "I'd better go. The nurse who's giving me a tour of the hospital probably thinks I got lost."

"Keep your head up, Dr. Gordon. And believe that everything is working in your favor."

"It doesn't feel that way, but okay. I'll let you know how things go."

Eva disconnected the call and stared at the wall, forcing down the lump of despair creeping up her throat. She stood on wobbly legs, making her way to the ER while praying she wouldn't run into Clark again. Once there, Brandi handed her a lab coat.

"Here you go, Dr. Gordon. You never know. We may have to step in and lend a hand during the middle of the tour. So it's best to be prepared."

"From the looks of things," Eva replied, jumping back as paramedics flew past her with a stretcher in tow, "that seems very likely."

The waiting area was filled with weary-looking patients, sitting among worried friends and relatives. A security guard waved his hands in the air while struggling to organize a large group of people swarming the reception desk.

"Follow me," Brandi said. She led Eva down a long corridor while pointing from side to side. "These are our areas of care. From the resuscitation and trauma units to the operating rooms and observation areas, this is where you'll be spending the majority of your time."

Eva slowly pivoted, taking it all in. "Wow. This is so much different from what I'm used to."

"Let's head to the back. I'll show you where the library and prayer room are located. And don't worry. You'll adjust to this place in no time. I'm sure Dr. Malone will be more than happy to take you under his wing."

I highly doubt that... Eva mused, smiling through her apprehension while still rethinking her decision to come to Las Vegas.

CHAPTER TWO

"UM… CLARK?" LEO ASKED, rushing to catch up with him. "What was *that* all about?"

"Nothing I wanna talk about."

Clark could barely see through the blur of disbelief clouding his vision. Thoughts of Eva filled his head. She was the woman he'd once called his best friend. Whom he'd accidentally fallen in love with. Who'd then proceeded to break his heart.

And who is now going to be my colleague for the next three months. What the hell?

He stormed inside Leo's office and grabbed a stack of patient files off the cluttered desk.

"Where is Mr. Johnson's chart?" he barked.

"The triage nurse has it. Dude, what is wrong with you?"

Clark ignored the question as memories of med school flashed through his mind. Memories he'd struggled to forget, of all the times he and Eva had sat on the beige-carpeted floor of her studio apartment, venting about classroom woes and family drama, or past heartbreaks and future dreams. Through it all, their bond had intensified. So had Clark's feelings. But he'd resisted the urge to act on them during their first couple of years, afraid of ruining the friendship.

Their third year, however, he broke, no longer able to restrain his emotions. That sensual evening they'd spent together had been electrifying, filling Clark with hope. He was convinced they'd finally take things to the next level and had broached the subject of dating exclusively.

But Eva's head was in a different space. Clinicals, passing the boards and landing the perfect residency were her primary focus, leaving no room for a relationship. Her decision to remain friends pained Clark. For him, reverting back to the way things were, as though nothing had happened, had been impossible. He'd been down that road once before and already knew how the story would end—just as it had with his high school sweetheart, Jessica Hardwick.

Clark and Jessica had dated throughout their teenage years. After the pair graduated from Chicago's St. Pierius High School, he'd looked forward to maintaining a long-distance relationship as she went off to college in Georgia and he'd headed to Michigan.

But Jessica had other plans. She wanted to be single while exploring her new life in Atlanta. Clark had objected, insisting that their relationship was too solid to just throw away. Jessica, however, disagreed.

"Come on, let's live a little," she'd said. "See who else may be out there for us. We'll always be the best of friends. And if we're meant to be, trust me, the universe will bring us back together."

Clark had no choice but to let her go. Just as he'd suspected, once the pair went their separate ways, the connection had crumbled. Jessica's calls, texts and emails slowly subsided, while his went unanswered. The visits she'd promised never happened. After pledging a sorority and joining the student body government, that was it. Jessica cut him off completely and moved on.

The experience had left Clark feeling extremely cautious. He spent the rest of his college years casually dating, refusing to allow himself to get hurt again. Whenever a woman attempted to get serious or mentioned settling down, he'd walked away, determined to safeguard his emotions.

Then along came Eva. The only one who was able to shatter his shield of protection. It was as if he had no control over his own feelings. The power she'd had over him was frightening, but equally exhilarating. For the first time in a long time, Clark dropped his guard and let her in, even sharing what he'd gone through with Jessica. Despite knowing Eva was focused more on her goals than a relationship, that night they'd slept together had prompted him to put his heart on the line, only to be hurt once again. Since then, Clark's heart had remained firmly under lock and key. And he had no plans to release it.

Beep!

The hospital's blaring intercom jolted him out of his thoughts.

Pull yourself together...

"I'll be back," Clark told Leo. He charged out of the office and into the ER, approaching the triage nurse. "Is Mr. Johnson still here, or has he been transferred to the ICU?"

"He's still here. We're waiting for a bed to become available in intensive care. But don't worry, he's stable. Nurse Collins is in with him now."

"Good. I'll go check on him."

Footsteps pounded behind Clark as he headed to the trauma unit.

"Hey!" Leo called out. "Wait up. There's something I want to ask you."

Clark threw his hand in the air. "Please don't start with the line of questioning. It's already been a long day and I'm running on fumes. We've treated four heart attacks, three strokes, a couple of near-fatal car accident victims and an overdose. All before noon."

"Well, they don't call Las Vegas the city that never sleeps for nothing. The action doesn't cease. Neither do the injuries and illnesses. But wait." Leo stopped Clark in the middle of the hallway. "Are you running on fumes because of work? Or because you were out late last night with Veronica?"

Clark opened Mr. Johnson's chart, focusing on the myocardial infarction victim's vitals rather than his friend's curious stare. "Didn't I just tell you not to start with the questions?"

"You did. But I figured you were referring to Eva. Not Veronica. So come on. Spill it. I already know things must've gone well considering she made it all the way to a fifth date. That's a record for you, isn't it?"

Clark ignored him.

"Okay, just answer this question. Do you think Veronica is the one? Because judging by what you've told me, she sounds phenomenal."

"She is phenomenal. But here's a better question. Am I even *looking* for the one?"

Leo's dark green eyes rolled into the back of his shiny bald head. "If you're not, you should be."

Clark fell silent.

"Oh, no." Leo sighed.

"Oh, no, what?"

"You've got that look on your face."

"What look?"

"That little scowl you get every time one of your flings has fizzled out. You and Veronica are over, aren't you?"

"I wouldn't say we're over," Clark rebutted, "because that would imply we were actually in a relationship to begin with. Veronica and I agreed to keep things casual from the start, which we did. Now we're both ready to move on."

Leo crossed his arms over his potbelly. "You're both ready? Or *you're* ready?

"You know," he continued without giving Clark a chance to respond, "for such a smart, cool, good-looking guy, you're a lost cause. Why were you ready to move on, exactly? Wait, let me guess. I bet you pulled the whole *I'm a busy physician* spiel. Claimed you work long hours and don't have much free time."

"That's exactly what I did. Because it's true. And guess what? Veronica, who is a smart, beautiful, in-demand entertainment attorney, understood completely. She doesn't have much free time on her hands, either. So there were no hard feelings. We do enjoy each other's company, though. If we ever wanna get together again, the door is open."

"Most men would kill to date a woman like Veronica. Yet here you are, ending things yet again. What is the problem?"

"There is no problem," Clark replied matter-of-factly while approving Mr. Johnson's prescriptions for amlodipine, metoprolol and atorvastatin. "Because I only date women who are looking for something casual. Fun. Nothing too serious. Thus far, that's working out just fine for me."

"I disagree, man. Having the right woman in your life—*one* woman—would only make you better."

"Why is it always the single ones dishing out the most advice?"

Leo snorted loudly. "Hold on now. Let's not forget, I wasn't always single. I'm speaking from experience. I learned my lesson the hard way. It wasn't until my ex-wife left me that I realized how wonderful it is to have a great partner by your side."

"Point taken. Now let's end this conversation. I've got patients to see."

Clark continued down the hallway and stepped inside Mr. Johnson's room. Nurse Collins was hovering over the side of the bed. She looked up and held a finger in the air.

"Hey, Doc," she whispered. "I just need a few more minutes. I'm inserting Mr. Johnson's catheter. Once I check his vitals and change his IV, I'll go over his chart with you."

Clark gave her a thumbs-up before quietly slipping out.

"Nowhere to run to now, is there?" Leo taunted, his thin lips spreading into a Cheshire cat grin. "I think it's time that we get to the bottom of your commitment issues."

Clark brushed past him and posted up at a mobile workstation. Just as he opened Mr. Johnson's health record, his cell phone pinged. A notification appeared from one of his various dating app accounts.

You have a new private message!

Leo peered over his shoulder, staring at the screen. "You're already back on a dating app trying to meet someone new, aren't you?"

"Mind your business, Director Graham."

"That's hard to do when you make it so obvious. I recognized the sound of that ping. It's an alert from Two of Hearts."

"How do you even know that?"

"Because I'm a platinum member myself."

"Of course you are." Clark handed him the phone. "Now that the cat's out the bag, check out Kelsie's profile. She's a dancer at the Bellagio hotel. According to her message, she's interested in becoming a doctor and wants to pick my brain."

Leo stared at the screen, shaking his head while swiping through the photos. "She's gorgeous. But judging by the looks of her expensive shopping sprees and fancy nights out on the town, Kelsie isn't interested in becoming a doctor. She's interested in *landing* one."

"Hater," Clark quipped, snatching the phone back and replying to the message.

I'd love to get together with you and discuss my work as a physician. Are you free for drinks tonight?

Kelsie responded within seconds.

Hold, please. Let me check my schedule...kidding! Yes, I'm free. My rehearsal ends at eight p.m. How about we meet at the Bellagio's Baccarat Bar and Lounge at eight thirty?

That sounds good. I'll see you there. Looking forward to it.

Leo placed his hand on Clark's shoulder. "As a friend, I'm advising you to stop with all the serial dating and take some time to figure out what you're so afraid of. Truth be told, I already know what it is. You just need to admit it to yourself."

"Admit *what*?"

"That the stunning doctor we just ran into, who you are refusing to talk about, is the reason you're such a commitment-phobe."

Clark's mouth went dry. He racked his brain for a snappy response but came up empty.

"Dr. Eva Gordon," Leo pressed. "Also known as the one that got away. You may not realize this, but you talk about her all the time. I won't even get into how you stalk her social media."

"Oh, so now I'm a commitment-phobe *and* an online stalker?"

"I'm just calling it like I see it. Don't think I haven't noticed you scrolling through her Instagram from time to time. Isn't that how you found out she'd gotten engaged?"

The reminder made Clark's heart ache. He pulled up Mr. Johnson's chest X-rays and focused on his coronary calcium scan results, avoiding Leo's inquisitive gaze.

"Dr. Malone, please report to the ER reception desk. Dr. Malone to the ER reception desk."

"Ahh, saved by the bell," Leo said drily, following closely behind Clark as he trekked toward the front of the emergency room. "But don't think this conversation is over just because you've been called to the principal's office. Because it isn't."

Clark ignored his well-meaning yet irritating friend and entered the lobby. When he caught a glimpse of the front desk, he stopped abruptly.

"Wait!" he whispered, grabbing Leo's arm and pulling him back.

Leo yelped loudly after almost tumbling into the wall. "What is the problem now?"

"Eva and Brandi are at reception."

"*Okay.* They're probably the ones who called for you. Why don't you go find out what they want?"

Clark didn't budge as the tremors in his feet shot straight to his gut.

"Ugh, how do I say this?" Leo sighed, staring up at the ceiling. "I know the subject of Eva is off-limits. But come on, she's going to be working here for the next three months. Avoiding her will be impossible. You need to resolve these issues that you have, *quickly*. Maybe even try to reestablish the friendship. Better yet, rekindle the relation—"

"All right," Clark interrupted. "Don't get ahead of yourself. Come on. Let's get this over with."

His limbs transformed into cement as he dragged himself through the waiting area.

Deep breaths, Clark thought, only managing to pull thin streams of air through his constricted lungs. The closer he got to Eva, the faster his pulse raced.

"Las Vegas," Leo muttered. "Also known as the city of second chances. Gotta love it…"

Brandi gave the men a thumbs-up as they approached. "Dr. Gordon and I just finished our tour of the hospital. I was hoping the two of you could give her a more in-depth look at the ER, maybe discuss some of the things that she can expect to encounter while working here at Fremont General."

All eyes turned to Clark. He was silent, still stunned by the fact that Eva was in his presence. While he just stood there, blinking rapidly in search of something valuable to contribute, Leo stepped forward.

"Well, one thing I can tell you is that here in Las Vegas, there isn't much you *won't* see inside the ER."

"Now that is a fact," Brandi added.

Clark looked on as the threesome bantered back and forth, hating himself for freezing up. But the idea of Eva being thrust back into his life so suddenly, so unexpectedly, had thrown him off his game. Rather than join the conversation, he remained motionless, quietly taking it all in.

Eva had somehow managed to become even more beautiful than she'd been years ago. Her toned, curvy figure proved she hadn't missed many gym days. Those wide-set eyes, with their dazzling hazel specks, could put the coldest soul in a trance. And those lush lips, the top one puckering slightly over the bottom, ignited memories of them wrapped around his—

"So, Dr. Gordon," Leo said, his booming voice disrupting Clark's lustful thoughts. "Where were you working before coming to Fremont General?"

"A small medical clinic in Black Willow, Iowa."

"Huh, interesting. And you left Black Willow behind for *Las Vegas* of all places?"

Eva hesitated, her eyes shifting as she pulled

a stray brunette curl behind her ear. "Yes, that's right."

"But what about your fian—?"

"You know," Clark interjected, grabbing Leo's arm, "what I think Leo's trying to say is that Las Vegas is quite a switch-up from such a small community. Nothing you can't adjust to, I'm sure, Dr. Gordon. Have you uh…have you found a place to stay yet?"

"I have. I'm staying at the Cascade Tower. It's not too far from here."

"I'm familiar with that complex. It's really nice. I lived there for a while when I first moved to Vegas—"

The conversation was interrupted when a team of paramedics came rushing through the door. As the group turned toward the entrance, Leo leaned toward Clark, whispering, "There's trouble in small-town paradise between Eva and the fiancé. Mark my words."

"We'll talk about it later."

Clark's attention was solely focused on the distressed patient being wheeled in on a stretcher.

"It hurts," the man yelled, writhing against the mattress. "It *hurts*!"

Clark jumped into action, charging toward the EMTs. Brandi and Eva followed closely behind.

The patient's entire face was charred, and patches of hair had been burned off his scalp. His navy blue T-shirt was tattered, and the white jeans barely hanging from his blackened legs were scorched. The skin on his arms, torso, chest and neck was covered in burn wounds that oozed blood from the raw inner layers.

"Talk to me," Clark said, leading the group toward the trauma area. "What happened to our patient?"

"We've got a severe burn victim," a paramedic panted. "Second or third degree judging by the leaking fluid and black center encased within majority of the wounds. There's deep partial thickness. We tried to dress the wounds before leaving the scene, but the patient wouldn't allow it. So we covered him in sterile burn sheets instead. We've been monitoring his airway and it doesn't appear compromised, so we don't believe intubation will be necessary. All other vitals are stable. We also established an IV to help with the pain management—"

"Pain management?" the patient shrieked as they wheeled him inside room 7. "Every inch of my body is stinging like hell!"

"What is your name, sir?" Clark asked, quickly washing his hands, then slipping into personal protective equipment. He glanced over at Eva and Brandi. They were both pulling on surgical masks and gloves.

Just as I remember, he thought of Eva. *Always ready to jump in and help however she could...*

"Sir, what is your name?" Clark repeated after getting no answer the first time.

"Fr-Frank. Frank Rojas."

"Nice to meet you, Mr. Rojas. My name is Dr. Malone. My colleagues and I are going to take good care of you, okay? Now, can you tell us how this happened?"

"I—I don't wanna talk about it. Just fix me up so I can get the hell out of here."

Mr. Rojas emitted an excruciating howl. Paramedics positioned the stretcher next to the hospital bed, and on the count of three, transferred him while disconnecting the EMS monitor.

Medical team members swarmed about the room. But Clark's eyes were focused on only one—Eva. She had teamed up with Brandi and Rian, the surgical technician, to gather sterile saline mist and moist gauze.

"We should we set up an IV for fluids to prevent dehydration and organ failure," Eva said.

Even in a totally new environment, she's still a boss...

Clark gave her a reassuring nod. Business first. Despite their rocky past, he wanted her to feel at ease now that she was a part of his hospital's staff. "Good idea, Dr. Gordon." He grabbed a pair of scissors and began cutting away at Mr. Rojas's clothing while speaking to the paramedics. "Do you all have the details on how this happened?"

"According to the patient's friends, he was sitting in the back seat of a car setting off fireworks."

"I-I'm sorry. He was doing *what*?"

"Setting off fireworks inside a car."

"Ahh!" the patient screamed. "Don't remind me."

"Mr. Rojas, how is your eyesight?" Clark asked, grabbing an ophthalmoscope from the custom procedure tray. "Are you able to see clearly?"

"I guess," he rasped. "It's blurry. So blurry…"

Clark switched on the instrument's light, adjusted the diopter dial and peered into the patient's eyes through the viewing window.

Mr. Rojas screamed out in pain. "What is that? It's excruciating! I can see, *dammit*. I can see!"

"I'm sorry, sir. I just need to check for any damage to your eyes."

Eva approached, picking up an otoscope and checking the patient's ears. "Do you detect any injuries thus far?"

"Not as many as I'd expect considering the circumstances. There's a bit of bleeding in the right eye. But no ruptures, burns or abrasions. No retinal detachments, either. How are his ears looking?"

"There's some redness and minor blistering. I'm not noticing severe burns or fluid buildup."

"Good. That's nothing a little ofloxacin otic solution can't fix." Clark set the ophthalmoscope on the procedure tray, his hand brushing against Eva's as she returned her instrument. They both quickly pulled away, glancing at each other apologetically. But he couldn't ignore the tingle shooting up his arm.

Stay focused...

"Mr. Rojas," he said, "further testing will need to be done on your vision and hearing. But the fact that they're both still intact after what you've been through means you're one lucky man."

The patient moaned, giving Clark a feeble thumbs-up.

Brandi began administering the IV just as Rian brought over the solution and gauze. Together, Clark and Eva began treating Mr. Rojas's burns.

Eva shifted from wound to wound, cleaning and wrapping while comforting the patient. Her seamless movements sent a jolt of electricity up Clark's side. He was reminded of moments they'd shared during medical school, adjusting to being out of the classroom and on the ward together. The invaluable time during clinical rotations and studying for the Step Two CK exams had created an inexplicable bond between them. Which is what ultimately led to that night...

You're doing it again... Focus!

"Dr. Malone," Eva said, "take a look at the index finger on the patient's right hand. There's a significant amount of burnt tissue."

Clark studied the dark, stiff mass. "Looks like

eschar, a result of the circumferential skin burns. If we don't take care of that now, the accumulation of extracellular and extravascular fluid will cause the tissue to lose its viability."

"I'm thinking we should perform an—"

"Emergency escharotomy," the pair said in unison.

"Great minds," Brandi told them. "I bet you two were a force to be reckoned with during your med school days. I can tell by the way you work together so effortlessly."

Eva nodded and Clark followed suit, not quite knowing how else to respond. He kept his eyes on Mr. Rojas's injury, palpating the finger and wrist, then pointing to an area that was severely scarred.

"Feels like there's some extreme stiffness running all the way across the wound. But his pulse is strong. Rian? Can you gather the tools needed for an escharotomy?"

"You got it."

Eva positioned Mr. Rojas's arm at a ninety-degree angle with the palm facing upwards. She cleaned the wound with chlorhexidine solution and swathed the area with sterile surgical drapes. "Lidocaine, please?"

Rian handed her the local anesthesia, which she quickly applied to the unburnt skin. While waiting for the numbing effect to take hold, Eva continued treating the remaining burns on Mr. Rojas's body alongside Brandi.

It was difficult for Clark to take his eyes off her. The thought of Eva being there for the next three months thrashed through his mind. Moments ago, he was being badgered by Leo over their lingering issues. Then next thing he knew, *boom!* She was working right next to him in the ER. Life could be funny.

And painful. So don't forget the past and keep your head on straight. This is just business...

Clark used a surgical marker to designate the area where he'd initiate the incision, then placed a scalpel near the top of the wound. "I'm going to begin the incision here, cutting one centimeter longitudinally into the healthy subcutaneous tissue so that the finger can swell without constricting the underlying blood vessels."

"Which will hopefully avoid amputation," Eva murmured.

"Exactly." Clark skillfully carried the incision through the deep partial thickness of the skin, watching as the dead tissue separated. The subcutaneous layer of fat, located just beneath the skin, immediately split, indicating the pressure had been relieved.

"Excellent job, Doctor," Eva said, nodding her head. "That hardened tissue should soften up in no time."

Clark sucked in a deep breath of air, his chest

swelling from the compliment. Considering Eva graduated top of their class, he didn't take the statement lightly.

"Thank you, Dr. Gordon." He ran his finger along the incision in search of constricted areas. There were none. "The blood appears to be flowing properly, which will allow for adequate ventilation. Can you please hand me the—"

"Of course," Eva interjected, grabbing a bundle of sterilized impregnated gauze soaked in bacitracin.

"See, that's what I'm talking about," Brandi said. "You two make a great team. Dr. Gordon, looks to me like I was right. You'll adjust to Fremont General's ER just fine."

"Let's hope so."

Clark could feel Eva's eyes on him. *Deflect*, he thought, quickly dressing the wound, then turning to Brandi. "We need to arrange for Mr. Rojas to be transferred to the burn unit."

"Leo said he would reach out and let them know we have a patient coming their way."

"Great. Rian, can you follow up and find out if a room is ready? As long as Mr. Rojas's vitals remain stable, he can be moved there."

"I'm on it."

"I love the teamwork around here," Eva said. "As hectic as things are, everyone does their part to make sure it all flows smoothly."

"That's the beauty of Fremont General," Clark

said. "There's a camaraderie that you won't find in too many other hospitals. I've been told that by several of the temporary employees who've come and gone. Plus, you'll never get bored. I'm assuming this is a far cry from your typical day in a Black Willow ER."

"*Far cry* would be an understatement. The last patient I saw before moving here was a Little Leaguer who'd fractured his elbow during practice. And he was one of only four patients I treated that day."

"Well, the experience you'll get here will be incredible," Brandi chimed in. "That Black Willow ER will be even more of a breeze once your temp assignment is up and you return home."

Hearing Brandi speak of Eva leaving sent a wave of sadness mixed with regret and disappointment through Clark. The flurry of emotions triggered another reminder to keep his distance and focus on instating a platonic working relationship with Eva.

He turned toward the monitor, focusing on Mr. Rojas's vitals rather than his own baffling reaction. The patient was stable. He'd been calm for the past fifteen minutes, indicating the pain medication had finally set in. Clark examined his body from head to toe. Each of his burns had been treated and wrapped securely.

"Good work, everyone," Clark said briskly.

"Dr. Gordon, thank you for diving right in and lending us your expertise. You were great."

"Thanks. That's what I'm here for."

Brandi tapped Eva's shoulder. "Doctor, the hospital administrator just paged me. You're twenty minutes late for your meeting."

"Oh!" Eva glanced at her watch. "I was so caught up in the moment that I forgot all about it." She turned to Clark. "It…um…it was good seeing you again, Dr. Malone. I'm looking forward to us working together."

"Same here. This was pretty nostalgic. Brought back some fond memories." He paused, reflecting on the not-so-fond memories her presence had brought on as well. The thought darkened his expression.

Eva removed her mask, revealing a bright smile. She stared at Clark, as if waiting for him to say more. Instead, he abruptly turned to Rian.

"Did you speak with Leo?"

"I did. The burn unit is prepared to receive Mr. Rojas whenever he's ready. Should I put in a call to patient transportation?"

"Yes, please. Thank you."

"Ready to head over to the administrator's office?" Brandi asked Eva, whose eyes were still on Clark. Her smile had faded and eyes dimmed. He figured she'd sensed his shift in demeanor. But he couldn't help himself. It was an honest reaction to their tumultuous past. He had to protect himself.

"Yes," she uttered quietly, slowly backing away. "I'm ready."

"Hey," Brandi said, "why don't we all get together for drinks after work? It would be a nice way to end this chaotic day. *And* an official welcome to Las Vegas gathering for you, Dr. Gordon. I'll invite Leo, and we can hit one of our favorite wind-down spots, the Oasis. How does that sound?"

"Sounds good to me," Eva said, her tone tinged with apprehension as she focused on Clark. "But what about you, Dr. Malone? Would you be comfortable with that?"

He hesitated.

It's just drinks. Can't hurt. As long as your head stays on straight and you keep your distance.

"Yes, I'm fine with that. My shift ends at six. See you shortly thereafter?"

"See you then."

Clark watched as the pair walked out of the room. His eyes gravitated toward Eva's swaying hips and shapely legs. The stirring below his belt quickly turned him back around.

"Reel it in…" he muttered, already feeling himself starting to unravel.

In that moment, Clark made a promise to himself to remain professional, but keep his guard up. Because when it came to Eva, being vulnerable would lead him right back where he was all those years ago—hurt and filled with regret.

CHAPTER THREE

EVA PULLED IN front of the Oasis and handed her keys to the valet. She felt like the new kid at school, walking into the homecoming dance alone, as nervous energy surged through her veins.

This is a bad idea. I should've stayed back at the apartment and finished unpacking.

A tsunami of emotions swirled through her head. She still hadn't fully processed the surprise reunion with Clark. The reaction seemed mutual, with him appearing just as stunned. At times, Eva sensed that he was very wary of her. Looking back, she wished she would've clarified where she stood before their steamy night together and made sure they were on the same page. Because then perhaps Clark would not have walked away afterward so hurt, to the point that it had cost them their friendship.

But once the burn victim arrived in the ER, she and Clark had fallen right back in sync with each other. It was as if they hadn't skipped a beat since their days of joint clinicals. The chemistry between them was still evident, and as far as Eva could tell, so was the attraction.

When she was leaving the ER, however, things took a strange turn. Clark suddenly turned cold. Eva was shocked he'd even agreed to drinks.

Just keep things light tonight. You're here to work. Not struggle to get back into Clark's good graces.

Eva entered the rustic bar, immediately realizing she'd overdressed. Her violet silk blouse and black pencil skirt stuck out in a sea of tank tops, denim shorts and flip-flops.

"Over here, Dr. Gordon!"

She spun around and waved at Brandi, who was tucked away in a corner booth near the DJ's station. Leo was sitting across from her, bopping his head to the beat of a nineties dance track. Clark was nowhere in sight.

Maybe he decided not to come after all.

Eva made her way over to the other side of the lounge, struggling not to stumble as her patent stilettos sank into the grooves of the cracked hardwood floor.

"Hey," Leo said. "Glad you could make it."

"Thank you for inviting me." She took a seat next to Brandi. "I really needed this after the day we had."

Brandi slid a plate of nachos in front of her. "Tell us about it. The Oasis has become somewhat of a savior. We've spent so many evenings here in this very booth, recouping and venting over—"

"Rounds of vodka martinis," someone said. *Clark.*

A slight flutter flowed through Eva's chest as he approached with drinks in hand. He appeared slightly overdressed as well, albeit extremely handsome, in his pale blue button-down shirt, slim-fitting navy slacks and Italian loafers.

Clark set the cocktails on the table, then handed one to Eva.

"An old-fashioned for you, assuming it's still your favorite."

His lips formed a slight smile, revealing the deep dimple in his left cheek. The flutter in Eva's chest morphed into full-blown palpitations.

"You remembered. And yes, old-fashioneds are still my favorite. Thank you."

Clark slid into the seat directly across from her. "Of course I remembered. That was your drink of choice all throughout med school."

Leo snorted, his gaze bouncing back and forth between the pair. "So, Dr. Gordon. We didn't get a chance to talk much back at the hospital. I know you're here in Vegas by way of Iowa. How did that happen?"

The question stiffened Eva's spine. She sat straight up, debating exactly how much she should share.

"Please, call me Eva. And um… I was just looking for a change of scenery. And pace, obviously. Things can get a little slow in a small-town ER. I figured coming to Vegas would offer up an invaluable experience that I could take back to my colleagues."

"Yep," Leo replied. "This could very well be the experience of a lifetime for you."

Eva noticed Clark throw him a sharp look. Leo slumped down in his seat, avoiding Clark's glare while burying his face in his drink.

"Here's what I'd like to know," Brandi said. "How many patients have you treated in Black Willow who've let off fireworks inside a car?"

"Not one. I must say, that was a shocker."

"Only in Vegas," Clark said with a smile that quickly faded when Leo chimed in again.

"So, hold on, Eva. Is that the *only* reason you left Black Willow? To gain experience?"

What is with this guy?

"Yes," she replied firmly. "It is."

"Well, whatever the reason," Brandi interjected as if sensing the strain, "we're just happy to have you here."

The DJ turned down the music and hopped on the mic.

"Hello, hello, hello, my party people!" he shouted.

Eva relaxed against the back of the booth, grateful for the interruption.

"Welcome to Benny B.'s Bodacious Cocktail Hour. I hope you're enjoying the half-priced drinks and bottomless baskets of buffalo wings. In between all the sips and nibbles, be sure to hit the dance floor and groove to the beat of these old-school throwbacks."

Boom!

Eva jumped in her seat when a loud bass drum blasted through the speakers.

"Let's *go!*" Benny B. yelled.

Montell Jordan's "This Is How We Do It" began to play. The crowd rushed toward the middle of the lounge.

"Leo!" Brandi squealed. "This is our song. Come on. Let's dance!"

The words were barely out of her mouth before he hopped up, grabbed her hand and led her to the dance floor.

Eva watched them shimmy away, tapping her fingernails against the table as nauseating jitters kicked in. She wasn't ready to be alone with Clark. The thought of him pulling her into an impromptu interrogation about their complicated past was worrying to say the least.

She glanced at him. He was staring into his glass, his soft, full lips curled around the rim. The sight sparked memories of his mouth pressed against her neck, her breasts, her stomach, her...

What are you doing? Stop it!

"So, how are your parents doing?" Eva asked, hoping to extinguish the heat rising inside her.

"Are they still sending you those amazing care packages like they used to back when we were in medical school?"

"Ha! I wish. They're both doing well. My father retired from his principal position at Wellington High School last year. But he hasn't been able to talk my mother into leaving her job at the Archway Art Center. She's teaching collage therapy to teens and senior citizens and loves what she's doing. I told him to just let her be. She'll retire when she's ready. What about Dr. and Mrs. Gordon? How have they been?"

"They're doing well. My dad is still running his practice, and my mom is heavily involved in her charity work and Black Willow's social scene."

"Nice. Glad to hear it." Clark pointed at her drink. "How's your old-fashioned? You've barely touched it."

"It's good. Strong, but good. They don't make them quite like this back home."

"Speaking of home, how is life there? Better yet, how's life in general? Since we…you know, lost touch."

The cool distance in his low tone tightened her throat.

Don't get too deep. Keep it simple.

"Life is pretty good. Not as exciting as Las Vegas, I would imagine. But I've got my family there, and a great group of friends. Remember Amanda Reinhart?"

"I do. Wasn't she on the ward with us during most of our rotations?"

"She was. Well, after graduation, she ended up moving to Black Willow and works at the clinic with me now."

"Uh-oh. The two of you, together again? Nothing but trouble. I sometimes wonder how that woman ever graduated considering how hard she used to party."

"Yeah, well, her days of partying are long gone. Amanda is married with two daughters now."

"Really? Wow. I didn't think settling down was in the cards for her." Clark hesitated, twirling the stem of his glass between his fingertips. "What about you? You didn't date much during med school. Did that change after graduation?"

Eva's jaws clenched at the mention of dating and med school in the same sentence. Would talk of their failed friendship be next?

"It did change. I had a couple of serious relationships. But…" She shrugged, downing a gulp of whiskey. "Wasn't meant to be, I guess."

Clark's forehead creased with confusion. "Wait, but I thought you were engaged…" His voice trailed off.

"I'm sorry," Eva said, leaning into the table. "You thought I was what?"

"Never mind. I don't know what I thought. Anyway, isn't it something how one or two decisions can change the course of your entire life?"

Eva studied Clark's expression. There was a confidence in his steely gaze that she'd never seen before. A strength to his posture that oozed self-assuredness. She was taken aback by his newfound swagger, yet more intrigued by this unfamiliar version of him than she was comfortable with.

Do not let this man pull you into a conversation you're not ready to have.

"What about you?" she asked, avoiding the question with a turn of the tables. "I imagine dating is difficult considering how frenzied life as a big-city ER physician must be."

"Not really. Time management is key. Work-life balance is important to me, so when I'm at Fremont General, I give it my all. Then when I'm away from the hospital, my personal life gets my undivided attention. I always make room for both. You may not be able to relate to that concept, though."

Ouch.

The jab left Eva at a loss for words. She sat silently, debating whether to let it go or snap back.

"You're doing that thing you do," Clark said.

"What thing?"

"Biting the inside of your cheek. You used to do that whenever you were deep in thought.

Or faced with a question you didn't want to answer. Speaking of which, you didn't answer my question."

Eva pressed her palms against the bench's hardwood surface, still failing to respond.

"Hey, relax," Clark said, running his fingertips across the top of her hand. "This isn't a cross-examination. It's just two old friends, catching up."

Confusion bubbled inside Eva's brain as his actions swung like a pendulum. One minute he was running hot, seemingly still attracted to her. Then he'd make a cool, pointed remark about their past. The turmoil left her wondering whether she belonged there in Vegas.

Of course you do. If for nothing else, maybe just to try to rekindle our friendship.

Eva held her glass to her lips, allowing the spicy bourbon to linger on her tongue before responding. "To answer your question, yes. I do understand the importance of creating a good work-life balance. Have I always maintained a healthy one? No, I haven't. But I've gotten much better at it over the years."

"*Humph.* Well, I'm sure there's some lucky man back in Black Willow who appreciates that."

It sounded more like a statement than an inquiry. Either way, Eva avoided the comment by slipping an ice cube inside her mouth.

"All right, y'all," the DJ crooned into the mic. "Time to switch things up for a minute. I know you're gonna remember this classic. If you're here with that special someone, then you'd better hit the dance floor right now, because this one's for you."

Shania Twain's "You're Still the One" came streaming through the speakers. On impulse, Eva reached out and grabbed Clark's arm. "Remember this? It was my go-to karaoke song!"

"I sure do. I probably still have the videos from every performance. You know I recorded all of them." He took her hand in his. "Come on. Let's dance."

Clark didn't wait for her to respond. Not that it was a question. It was a command that she gladly followed.

He led her toward the middle of the lounge. On the way there, Brandi and Leo breezed past them.

"We need a break!" Brandi said, swiping her frizzy bangs away from her damp forehead. "*And* a drink."

"You two hitting the dance floor?" Leo asked Clark.

"Yeah, man. This was Eva's theme song back in the day."

"This song? 'You're Still the One'? Seems to me like it could be the theme song for both of you. Especially now that you're—"

Clark gripped Leo's shoulder, promptly shutting him up. "Why don't you go take a load off?

Have another vodka martini." He turned to Eva. "Shall we?"

"Yes," she replied, side-eyeing Leo as he walked away. "Is he always in frat boy mode?"

"Not always. He's a good guy. Just gets a little overenthusiastic from time to time. But he means well."

Clark found an empty corner on the packed dance floor and wrapped his arms around Eva's waist. She tentatively leaned into him, clasping her hands against the back of his neck while trying not to inhale the scent of his cedarwood cologne.

Their bodies swayed to the rhythm of the music. When he pulled Eva closer, her nipples stiffened against his chest. The sensation sent a back-arching quiver straight through her.

"Are you okay?" Clark murmured, his lips lightly caressing her earlobe.

"Mm-hmm," was all she could muster. Anything more and she might've climaxed right there on the dance floor.

Being nestled in his embrace felt intoxicating. She realized uncomfortably it was a thrill she hadn't felt with Kyle in quite a long time, if ever. Their heads swiveled simultaneously, bringing their lips together for just a brief moment. Eva attempted to pull away and apologize. But she couldn't move an inch within his tight grip.

Clark's firm hands glided down the sides of

her body, each finger savoring every curve before they rested on her hips.

Keep this up and you might have to come home with me, the potent old-fashioned was beckoning her to say.

A startling buzz vibrated against Eva's thigh. She stepped back while Clark reached inside his pocket.

"Sorry," he muttered. "Somebody's texting me."

The heightened sense of arousal rising inside Eva deflated suddenly. The backlash of emotion sent her thoughts reeling toward Kyle again, guiltily wondering how she'd gotten sucked back into Clark's charms so quickly when she was supposed to be heartbroken over her ex-fiancé.

She waited while Clark grabbed the phone and opened the message. Her eyes roamed toward the screen. Despite the tinted protector, she could still read the text. It had been forwarded from the Two of Hearts dating app.

Hello, handsome. My rehearsal ended early. I'm heading to the bar now. Can't wait to meet you. See you soon. Kelsie XO

Clark looked up at Eva. She quickly turned away, hoping he hadn't noticed her snooping.

"Sorry to cut the evening short," he said curtly,

"but I have to get going. I've got another engagement."

"No worries," she told him, almost choking on the lie. She'd allowed herself to get caught up in the moment, and just like that, some woman named Kelsie had brought her right back to reality. "I should probably get going, too. I've still got some unpacking to do."

Eva's shoulders slumped at the thought of going back to the corporate apartment, alone no less, with its cold hospitality furniture and pretentious neighbors. A chill swept over her when she and Clark headed back to the table. He didn't appear nearly as disappointed as she felt while he was saying his goodbyes, which were accompanied by smiles and embraces. The thought of him happily leaving her to go and see another woman sent an inexplicable stab of jealousy straight through her gut.

Don't go, Eva wanted to tell him just as Shania sang out about how far they'd come.

Before she knew it, Clark was out the door.

"Another round, Eva?" Brandi asked.

"I'd better pass. It's been a long day, and I'm still feeling a little jet-lagged. I should probably go since I have to be back at the hospital early in the morning. But thank you for inviting me."

"We'll have to do it again soon," Leo said, smiling slyly. "I'm glad you're here, Eva. I think your presence is going to have a great impact on Fremont General. In more ways than one."

The spark in his eyes ignited Eva's curiosity. She waited for him to elaborate. He didn't, instead turning to Brandi. "Another round for you, my friend?"

"Yes, please!"

Eva watched the pair nudge each other playfully. Suddenly, she began to feel like a third wheel. "I'll see you two tomorrow. Enjoy the rest of your evening."

"See you tomorrow, Eva!"

The moment Eva stepped outside, she was hit with a hard reminder.

You came here to work and mend your broken heart, not get entangled in a new situation.

But the chemistry between her and Clark was just as palpable now as it had been back in the day. Eva couldn't help but wonder whether Amanda was right, and this really was fate. Had the universe brought her to Las Vegas to reconnect with Clark?

The man who couldn't wait to leave and meet up with another woman?

That thought was all Eva needed to reel her emotions back in and push any romantic ideas of Clark out of her head. When a valet driver pulled her car to the curb, Eva handed him a tip, then collapsed into the seat, completely spent.

And just think. It's only day one...

CHAPTER FOUR

CLARK MADE HIS way through the Bellagio's casino. After taking a left turn past the Lily Bar and Lounge, the Baccarat Bar appeared up ahead. Clark's heart raced with anticipation. He was never this discombobulated before a first date. But tonight felt different. He couldn't seem to pull it together.

What in the hell is wrong with you?

A fresh sheet of sweat drenched his forehead.

Wiping it away, he thought, *You know exactly what's wrong. Dr. Eva Gordon.*

Clark still hadn't fully recovered from the moment he'd laid eyes on her outside the hospital cafeteria. While he had managed to perform alongside Eva inside the ER, seeing her at the Oasis had left him completely rattled. Especially after the seductive dance they'd shared. He couldn't lie to himself—it had felt far too good having her in his arms again. All those old feelings came rushing back, both physical and emotional.

I should've just canceled this date, Clark thought with a wince, his breathing quickening as he entered the bar area. *And stayed at the Oasis with—no!*

He gripped his forehead, attempting to pull the notion from his mind. Clark couldn't allow himself to forget what Eva had put him through. She'd left him high and dry back in the day, knowing how much he cared for her. Eva's goal of graduating top of their class and winning her father's approval were always her main priorities. Their friendship, and the possibility of there being something more between them, had seemed like an afterthought to her. That had hurt him beyond measure. Clark refused to open up to her again now and allow history to repeat itself. Not to mention Eva was on the rebound and probably didn't want to jump back into anything anyway.

You're thinking with your heart and not with your head. No backsliding. Stay focused. More importantly, keep your feelings in check...

Clark sucked in a puff of air, hoping the oxygen would shake his uneasiness. His roving eyes scanned a row of bright blue velvet barstools surrounding the circular gold bar. They landed on a woman sitting near the middle. Her long, toned legs were flung over the side of the stool. Her slender hand was wrapped around a martini glass filled with what appeared to be a lemon drop.

She flung her wavy jet-black hair over her shoulder and turned to him, smiling sexily as soon as their gazes connected.

This was the moment Clark had hoped would calm him. Seeing Kelsie sitting before him, not only matching her photos but looking even better in person, should've been reassuring. But instead of being overcome with excitement, he was hit with an anticlimactic feeling of disinterest.

She stood, pulling her shimmery cream tank dress down her thighs while sauntering toward him. The dress clung to her overflowing surgically enhanced breasts, tiny waist and curvy hips. Almost every man in the vicinity turned in her direction. Even a few of the women's heads swiveled. But Clark's vision was blurred by thoughts of Eva's body pressed against his as they swayed back and forth on the dance floor.

"Hello, Dr. Malone," Kelsie purred. She slid her hands along his chest, then rested them on his biceps. "It is so nice to meet you. And finally lay eyes on all this handsome, broad-shouldered glory."

"Nice to meet you, too," he croaked before clearing his throat. "Please, call me Clark."

"Okay, *Clark*."

She grabbed him by the hand and led him to an empty barstool. "I took the liberty of ordering you a lemon drop martini. They're my fave. Hopefully they're yours, too."

He hated lemon drops but didn't have the heart to tell her. "That's fine, thanks. I hope I didn't leave you waiting for too long."

"Not at all. I just hung out with a couple of the other dancers to pass the time. I actually saw you walking through the casino, so I dismissed them before you got to the bar. I didn't want the competition hanging around, if you know what I mean!"

Kelsie threw her head back and unleashed a cackle so loud that several patrons turned and stared.

Shifting in his seat, Clark emitted a forced chuckle. "So, which show do you perform in here?" he quickly asked in hopes of distracting her.

She took a long gulp of her drink. "Whew! Maybe I shouldn't have ordered this fourth martini. Sorry, did you say something?"

Fourth?

"Yes. I asked which show you're a part of."

"Oh! Yeah, so I dance in the Mayfair Supper Club show. It is so good, Doc. The best in town, really. Our choreographers have worked with Janet Jackson, Nicole Scherzinger, *Dancing with the Stars*... You should come see it tomorrow night! But all eyes on *me*. None of the other girls. You got it?"

"Er... I'll need to check my calendar first."

He lurched when Kelsie's hand slid up his knee and settled near his groin.

"So, Dr. Matlock," she murmured, "enough about me. Let's talk about you. Remember how I was telling you that I'm interested in becoming a doctor?"

"I do," Clark muttered, scooting back in his chair. "And it's Malone, actually."

"Ma—*who*?"

"Malone. My last name is Malone. Not Matlock."

"Oh! My apologies, Doc. Anyway, inquiring minds wanna know what a day in the life of a physician is like."

"My days can be pretty hectic. I wake up at about five o'clock in the morning to make sure I get a workout in, then—"

He stopped when Kelsie squeezed his biceps approvingly. "Mm-hmm. And it shows…"

Normally, the touch from a beautiful woman would've sent quivers straight below his belt. Tonight, he felt nothing. Clark wanted to blame it on the alcohol he'd consumed at the Oasis. But deep down he knew the real culprit.

"Hey!" Kelsie squealed, waving her hand in the air. "Are you listening to me?"

"I—Sorry, could you please repeat that?"

"I was saying that I get it. You work out, and you're probably busy at the hospital all day. Since I'm considering entering into the medical field and I have a certain lifestyle to maintain, what type of salary could I expect to make as an ER doctor?"

In other words, what does your paycheck look like?

Clark turned away from Kelsie's curious stare and signaled the bartender. "A glass of sparkling water, please?"

"Is there something wrong with your martini?" she asked.

"No, it's fine," he lied, considering he hadn't even tasted it. "I actually went out for drinks with a few of my coworkers right before coming here, so I'm good for now."

"Aww, you're no fun!"

When his phone buzzed, Clark snatched it from his pocket, thankful for the interruption. It was a text from Leo.

What's up? How's the date going? We need to discuss whatever's going on between you and Eva. She left the Oasis shortly after you. Seemed pretty down once you were gone.

"Who is that texting us?" Kelsie joked, leaning over Clark's shoulder and peering at his cell.

He quickly slipped it back inside his pocket. "Just my director of emergency medicine checking in." He paused, suddenly overcome by the urge to cut the night short. Hearing the details of Eva being disappointed after he'd left the bar was way more interesting than a shallow date that wasn't going anywhere.

"Why am I getting the feeling that you're not really into me?" Kelsie asked.

Taking a long sip of water, Clark racked his brain for the right words. "It's not you. I've just had a long day and need to get some patient files over to my coworker. That's one thing I didn't share about being an ER doctor. Our work is never done."

"Humph, interesting…"

She slumped down in her stool and drained her glass. Clark wanted to apologize. He knew he hadn't been good company. But he couldn't get his head in the game because it was clouded with thoughts of Eva.

Kelsie raised her glass in the bartender's direction. He nodded and immediately began prepping another lemon drop martini.

"You seemed so enthusiastic when we were exchanging messages. But now that you're here, you're just, like…*blah*. Is it that you're more outgoing on an app than in person? Takes you a minute to open up to people?" she asked.

Clark shrugged despite knowing that wasn't the answer. "You know, that could be the case."

His cell buzzed with another text from Leo.

Dude, are you okay? At least let me know you're good and your date hasn't kidnapped you!

"Could you please excuse me while I respond to this text? It's another message from my co-worker."

"Go right ahead." She waved him off and pivoted in her chair, focusing on the casino floor.

Clark typed.

Not good. Kelsie and I aren't connecting on any level.

A woman that gorgeous and you're having trouble connecting? Sounds to me like your mind is elsewhere. And by elsewhere, I mean stuck on Eva.

Clark tucked the phone away and turned his attention back to Kelsie, who was busy chatting up a buff man sitting next to her wearing a cowboy hat and sleeveless plaid shirt.

"Sure, let's do it!" she said to him before hopping out of her stool. "But I'd better warn you. I'm a blackjack master." Before walking off, she threw Clark a tight side-eye. "I'm gonna go hit the casino floor for a bit. Can I meet you back here in fifteen minutes or so?"

"Or," the cowboy chimed in while tipping his hat, "your friend can join us if he'd like."

"Thanks for the invitation, but I think I'll pass. Actually, I need to get going. I've got some work to do."

"Suit yourself," the cowboy said before taking Kelsie's hand and leading her away from the bar. She turned and pointed in Clark's direction.

"Don't forget to pick up the tab before you leave!" she tossed over her shoulder.

Just as Clark opened his mouth to reply, the bartender slid the bill in front of him. It was close to three hundred dollars.

"Excuse me, but I think you've given me the wrong check."

"No, that's the right one. Kelsie and her girls had a few rounds before you got here. She told me that her date would cover it. That's you, right? The doctor, not the cowboy?"

Clark tossed his credit card down onto the silver tray without dignifying the question with a response. The minute he signed the check, he jetted out of the casino.

"You should've just stayed put at the Oasis," he told himself before calling Leo.

CHAPTER FIVE

Eva waved at a group of intensive care nurses on the way to the hospital's cafeteria. She hadn't slept well and needed an iced shaken espresso before stepping foot inside the ER.

Thoughts of Clark being out with another woman left her tossing and turning all night. She wondered whether he'd reminisced on those sensual moments they'd shared on the dance floor like she had. The way her fingers caressed the back of his neck. His hands, gripping her hips as his mouth grazed her ear. Their lips touching ever so slightly...

A warm sensation rushed through Eva as she turned the corner. She fanned her flushed face before entering the cafeteria and eyeing the long line of patrons crowding the Drip & Sip Coffee Stop. Her stomach dropped to her knees at the thought of running into Clark, who she'd heard stopped by the station for green tea every morning.

Relief hit after Eva scanned the group of customers and didn't see him. She wasn't ready to face Clark just yet. At least not until she'd downed her first cup of coffee.

"Hey!" someone chirped behind her.

Eva jumped, startled by the high-pitched voice.

"Ooh, sorry," Brandi said. "Did I scare you?"

"You did. But it's not you, it's me. I didn't get much sleep last night so I'm probably a little on edge. Nothing a little caffeine won't fix. Or make worse. I don't know. Either way, I need it."

"Sounds like you and I are in the same boat. Except my excuse is that I stayed out *way* past my bedtime. Leo and I were having too good a time to cut the night short. But you left the Oasis so early. Did you stop off somewhere else before going home?"

"No." Eva crossed her arms over her chest. "I guess I'm still adjusting to being in a new place. In a new city. Working at a new hospital. You know…"

Brandi's eyes narrowed as her lips formed a slight smirk. "Yeah, I think I do know."

She's onto me…

"So, you and Clark seemed to have had a good time last night."

Eva moved up in the line while twirling a button on her lab coat, thinking of a way to deflect considering she knew the exact direction Brandi was steering the conversation. "I think we all did. Like you said, the Oasis is a great place to kick back and unwind. And the drinks were incredible."

The gleam in her gaze told Eva that her response was not convincing.

"It would be nice if the four of us could turn drinks at the Oasis into a weekly thing," Brandi suggested. "My friends don't understand what I go through working in that ER. Decompressing over cocktails with you three would be fantastic because you all get it."

"That we do. Weekly drinks sounds like a good idea to me."

Eva's nonchalant tone totally contradicted the flutters inside her chest. While she appreciated the idea of a group outing, all she could focus on was getting to spend time with Clark outside the ER.

Just as the pair approached the counter, Brandi's phone buzzed.

"Clark wants to know if I can pick up a green tea for him. Hot today, not iced. He's in the middle of a sign-out with Dr. Abrams and doesn't want to disrupt the exchange of patient information. Oh, in case you didn't know, Clark can barely function without his morning dose of green tea."

"So I've heard. By the way, our morning fixes are on me today."

"Thanks, Eva!"

On the way to the ER, Brandi turned to Eva.

"Hey, can I ask you a question? And please stop me if I'm being intrusive."

"Of course. Ask away."

"What's the deal between you and Clark? Leo and I both picked up on the chemistry between you two, and it was giving more than just former classmates vibes. And again, feel free to tell me to mind my business if you don't want to answer that."

"No, you're fine," Eva replied while contemplating how much she should share. The soft expression on Brandi's face convinced her to come clean. "It makes sense that you two picked up on something, because Clark and I were really good friends during medical school. Then one night that friendship crossed over into something more. *Way* more. Afterward, Clark wanted to pursue a relationship while I thought it'd be best to remain friends and focus on our studies."

"Oh, wow. Were you able to maintain the friendship after that?"

"Unfortunately, no. We ended up drifting apart, then lost touch after graduation. So seeing him here in the ER was pretty shocking."

Brandi slowly nodded while taking a sip of her drink. "Interesting. That explains a lot."

"What do you mean?"

"Clark is somewhat of a serial dater. I've always wondered why he hadn't settled down considering he's such a catch. When I asked Leo about it, he reckoned he's still hung up on someone he'd gone to medical school with. Someone he'd loved deeply. *The one that got away*, as Leo always calls her, who'd turned Clark into a commitment-phobe. Sounds to me like that someone is you."

The sound of rattling ice filled the air. Eva glanced down, realizing it was her trembling hand shaking. Hearing that Clark may still have feelings for her sent her entire body into a fit of flurries.

But the sensation quickly fizzled once Eva realized that Leo must've been mistaken. Clark had been cool and distant toward her for the most part. And after the way he'd run off to meet up with another woman, she was sure that whatever feelings he may have had for her at one point were now long gone.

When they reached the ER, the doors swung open and Dr. Abrams came flying out. "Have a great day, ladies!" he huffed over his shoulder. "I'm late for my son's science fair presentation. Dr. Gordon, Dr. Malone will catch you up on the patient handoffs."

"Okay, thanks!"

Eva entered the emergency room, her eyes darting around the lobby in search of Clark.

Breathe, she thought, realizing she'd been holding a ball of air inside her chest. Just as she released an exhale, Clark appeared near the triage nurses' station. As if sensing Eva's presence, he glanced at her. His stern expression softened. He held a stack of patient files in the air and signaled her over.

"Clark probably wants to get started on the workups with you," Brandi said. "While you do that, I'll assess my patients and get their rooms stocked with supplies. Check in with you in a few?"

"Sounds good. Thank you."

As Eva headed toward the nurses' station, hot tea spilled over onto her hand. She'd been squeezing Clark's cup so tightly that liquid poured from the spout.

"Dammit," she hissed through clenched teeth.

Clark rushed over with tissues in hand, taking the cup, then gently patting down her fingers. The gesture brought back memories of how caring he'd always been. Had that been Kyle, he probably wouldn't have even looked up from whatever he was doing, let alone asked if she were okay.

What were you thinking when you let Clark go?

"Ooh," he uttered, "this cup is hot. Are you okay? Do you need me to grab some ice? Or antibacterial ointment?"

"No, no, I'm okay. That's actually your tea. I hope I didn't spill too much of it."

"I'm sure it's fine. Why don't I catch you up on

these medical charts before we make our rounds, start the workups, then check patients' test results?"

"Let's do it."

The pair headed down the corridor toward the trauma unit. Clark stopped at a mobile workstation and opened the chart at the top of his pile. "Bradley Turner was admitted last night after suffering a hemorrhagic stroke."

"Was it a subarachnoid or intracerebral hemorrhage?"

"Intracerebral. He was bleeding inside the brain."

Clark leaned into Eva, pointing at the notes section. "He suffered an ischemic stroke two years ago, which was pretty mild. Since then, he's sporadically taken his blood pressure medication and hasn't been keeping his diabetes under control. His labs show that he suffers from high cholesterol, which has gone untreated. We'll need to put together an ongoing treatment plan for him. For the time being, he's on losartan, furosemide, rosuvastatin and rapid-acting insulin. We'll see how his body reacts to those meds and make adjustments if necessary."

Focus on the chart. Not Clark's lips...

"Have his kidneys been affected?" she asked.

He flipped to the second page, his hand accidentally brushing against Eva's breasts in the process. She gasped slightly, not from the shock of it, but the shivers shooting through her chest. He continued obliviously as if not noticing a thing.

"According to his chart, they were. As of last night the patient's kidneys were functioning at forty-five percent. So we'll keep an eye on them."

"We should warn him that if he doesn't get his blood pressure, sugar levels and cholesterol under control, that function will continue to decrease. Let him know he'd be facing end-stage kidney failure and wind up on dialysis."

"Absolutely. We'll go over all of that with him. As for the rest of the patients…"

Clark shuffled through the remaining charts, briefing Eva on each of them as they moved farther along the unit. There was a new mother who'd given birth prematurely at almost seven months, a teen who'd overdosed on a mix of fentanyl and alcohol, and a pedestrian who'd been hit by a car and endured a concussion, shattered pelvis and dislocated shoulder.

"Those are the sickest patients we're dealing with right now," he continued. "Dr. Abrams has everyone else stabilized, so we'll check on those three first, then work our way through the rest of the rooms. Let's start with our stroke victim, Mr. Turner. I'll grab his most recent lab results."

Eva followed Clark to the nearest workstation. While he entered the patient number into the computer system, she felt the sudden urge to ask about his evening.

Don't do it. You are at work. Keep it professional. Plus, you're gonna be mad if he tells you it was great. So just leave it alone.

"How was the rest of your evening?" she blurted out.

The minute the words flew from her mouth, Eva wished she could reach into the air and snatch them back. But it was too late. Her stomach clenched as she anticipated his response.

Shrugging nonchalantly, Clark kept his eyes on the computer screen. "It was okay."

She waited for him to elaborate. Instead, he remained silent while pounding his index finger against the mouse.

Let it go. He obviously doesn't want to talk about it.

"Just okay?" Eva pressed, once again defying her inner voice. "I thought it would've gone better than that considering the way you rushed out of the Oasis…"

Her voice trailed off. She wanted to kick herself for saying too much.

"Put it this way," Clark replied drily. "I probably would've been much better off staying at the Oasis." His wide, inquisitive eyes scanned Eva's face. "What about you? How was the rest of your night?"

Miserable and sleepless, she wanted to admit.

But Clark didn't need to know how alone she'd felt, tossing and turning restlessly while wondering about his date.

"It was fine. I left shortly after you did. I was pretty exhausted."

"Hmm…okay." He turned his attention back to Mr. Turner's labs. The twitch in his lips told Eva that he wanted to say more but was holding back. His resistance left her longing for the days when they were close friends, able to share everything.

You have no one to blame for that but yourself.

"Okay," Clark said, grabbing a printout. "I've got Mr. Turner's lab results. Let's go check on him, then start the rest of our rounds. After that, we'll review the remaining patients' labs."

Clark moved from room to room with ease, treating each patient with kindness as he provided updates and care plans. Memories of making rounds together during medical school came flooding back to Eva, making it difficult to focus on the tasks at hand. Clark was just as charming now as he'd been back then. But his aura of complete confidence was new to her and only added to his charisma. Patients and their families alike grew enamored the moment he walked through the door. While it was a trait that most doctors didn't possess, he'd mastered it.

Eva prided herself on handling patients with great care. But after watching Clark, she realized there was room for improvement within her own process. His method of slowly reviewing charts and medication details, along with extensive conversations on wellness strategies post–hospital stays, were tactics that she'd definitely take with her when she left.

By the time the pair checked in with each patient on the floor, it was lunchtime. Eva expected to part ways with Clark and meet back up afterward. When he suggested they grab something together from the cafeteria, she was pleasantly surprised.

"Deb's Delicatessen has a really good turkey and Swiss on rye, and a delicious grilled chicken wrap, great avocado toast. But if you already have lunch plans, I understand. I just—I figured we could, you know, talk about the morning and go over plans for the afternoon, and—"

Placing a hand on his arm, Eva put a halt to Clark's rambling. "I don't have plans. Lunch with you sounds good."

His tense biceps relaxed against her palm. The reaction eased Eva's own angst slightly, making the idea of sharing a meal with him even more enticing.

But then fragments of anxiety crept through her mind as they headed to the cafeteria. How would the conversation go? Clark did say they'd be discussing work, but Eva suspected talk would drift to more personal matters, which, in their case, could be dangerous.

Just relax. You'll be fine...

She noticed a little bounce in his stride while strolling down the hallway. It became clear that Clark was Fremont General's resident celebrity. Practically everyone they passed, from doctors and nurses to transporters and custodians, greeted him with enthusiastic salutations and hearty waves.

"You are quite the superstar around here, aren't you?" Eva teased, his endearing response pulling at her heartstrings as she realized just how much of his growth she'd missed out on over the years.

"Nah, I wouldn't say that. But I will admit to being one of the friendlier doctors on staff."

Just as she looked down to adjust the clip on her ID badge, a stretcher came rushing toward them. Clark grabbed Eva by the waist and pulled her to the side. His hand lingered there well after the commotion had passed them by.

"You all right?" he asked.

"I'm fine," she breathed. "Thanks for pulling me out of the way. I almost ended up on top of that patient!"

He chuckled, guiding her back down the hallway. Eva's skin tingled underneath his touch as his hand slid down her hip. Overcome by a warm sense of comfort, she sensed their med school dynamic gradually beginning to resurface. His hot and cold vibes were tapering off, as was his wariness toward her. Eva wondered what had sparked the change in his behavior. Whatever the reason, she was grateful for it.

The twosome entered the cafeteria and made a beeline for the delicatessen. After Clark ordered their meals, they settled into a quiet booth tucked away in a corner.

"Thanks for treating me to lunch," she said. "You didn't have to do that."

"Don't mention it. I'm sure I owe you for something you did for me back in the day."

Slowly unwrapping her sandwich, Eva glanced up at Clark. "What's going on with you?"

"What do you mean?"

"Why are you being so nice to me?"

Leaning back in his seat, Clark crossed his arms over his chest in feigned shock. "When was I *not* nice to you?"

"Ha! We can start with the moment you laid eyes on me my first day here, then go down the list."

"Well, can you blame me? Never in my wildest dreams did I imagine reuniting with you of all people. *Here*. On my home turf. In all honesty, I'm still in shock over the idea of us working together." He paused, fiddling with the lid on his iced green tea.

"I could sense that. This was a shock to us

both. But…you know, reconnecting with you has been good. Awkward at times. But good."

"I agree." Wrinkles creased Clark's forehead. "I owe you an apology. I did have a couple of moments last night when I wasn't exactly kind."

"A couple," Eva quipped, before quickly adding, "Blame it on the alcohol?"

"As much as I'd love to blame it on the alcohol, I won't. Charge it to my bruised ego. I shouldn't have been so aloof, drilling you about our past then leaving abruptly on your first night in town. That's not something a friend would do."

"Oh, so we're friends again?"

"We're getting there…" Clark murmured through a sexy half smile.

"Well, I appreciate you saying that and accept your apology. Listen, why don't we start over from scratch? I know we can't erase the past, but we can agree to a clean slate while I'm working here. Not only would that be good for us, but it would be good for the patients and staff as well. How does that sound?"

"Like a plan."

"Good." Eva bit into her sandwich, attempting to take a cute, tiny bite as Clark eyed her across the table. The move proved to be an epic fail when a chunk of turkey fell to the floor and a glob of mayo hung from her lip.

"Oh, no," Eva choked out, scrambling for a

napkin. Within seconds, Clark had grabbed one and pressed it against her mouth.

"I guess some things never change, huh," she murmured.

"I guess they don't. Because look at me. Still looking out for you."

From the corner of her eye, Eva noticed Leo standing in line at the All-American Surf & Turf food stall. She hoped that he wouldn't interrupt her and Clark's conversation now that they were finally getting somewhere.

Clark followed her gaze, then grabbed his phone. After sending a text, he turned his attention back to his wrap. "So now that we've wiped the slate clean," he said, "let's start from the beginning. Have a *real* catch-up. What's life been like for you since med school?"

"Interesting, to say the least. And busy. I spend a lot of time at the clinic, and I'm involved in several charitable organizations. I, um—I was also…"

Just tell him.

"I'd been seeing someone for several years. We got engaged last year, but things didn't work out. So here I am. In Las Vegas."

Eva braced herself, expecting some sort of joke about how she was the one who'd probably ruined her engagement, or had run away when things got tough between her and Kyle. Surprisingly, Clark reacted with a look of sympathy.

"I'm sorry to hear that. And, since we're sharing, I have a confession to make."

He hesitated while watching the cafeteria's exit. Clark nodded slightly. Eva looked toward the door, watching as Leo waved, then walked out.

"Am I dreaming?" she asked. "Or did Leo actually pass up an opportunity to come over and socialize with us?"

"No, you're not dreaming. But in reality, it's because I just sent a text letting him know that we're in the middle of an important conversation."

"So in other words, just get your food and leave?"

"Exactly," Clark replied before the pair burst out laughing. "But look, back to what I was saying. Since we're opening up to each other, I have to tell you that I've kind of been keeping up with you over the years."

"Seriously? I thought you'd forgotten all about me after med school. It seemed as if you couldn't wait to get away from me."

"I couldn't. But not for the reasons you may have thought. I was still pretty hurt after the way things ended between us, hence me accepting a position across the country. But *forget* about you? I could never do that. We were too close for me just to push you out of my mind completely. As a matter of fact, I kept up with you through some of our classmates. And good ole social media, of course. That's how I knew you'd gotten engaged."

The confession almost knocked Eva out of her chair. "Wait, so you've known about that all this time?"

"I did. What I *didn't* know was that you and your fiancé had recently broken up. Hence my shock when I saw you here at the hospital, then found out you'd accepted a temp position in the ER."

A rumble stirred inside Eva's chest. After all this time, Clark still thought about her. Maybe Amanda was right. Maybe there was more to their serendipitous reunion than she'd thought.

Or more likely he just wants to rekindle your friendship. Don't go digging for something that's not there...

"What are you doing after work?" he asked.

"Unpacking. Why?"

"Why don't you put those boxes on hold and let me take you out? Show you around Las Vegas. Introduce you to the city the right way."

Eva's head tilted, her lips pulling into a smile. "Well, it wouldn't take much convincing for me to pass on the unpacking. So yes, I'd like that."

"Cool. Why don't we wrap up lunch and get back to the ER? We'll continue this conversation later tonight, outside of the hospital. I feel like we haven't even scratched the surface yet."

"We haven't. Because while you were all up in my business, I didn't get a chance to dig into yours. I can't wait to hear all about what you've been up since we lost touch."

"Uh-oh," Clark muttered, pushing away from the table. "And on that note, let's go."

As the pair headed out of the cafeteria, Eva felt lighter on her feet. Whether it was the fact that she and Clark had cleared the air or made plans for later, she was happy to have him back in her life.

CHAPTER SIX

"I DON'T APPRECIATE the way you dismissed me this afternoon," Leo barked when Clark entered his office.

"Look, don't start. I'm coming in here to apologize. Eva and I were having a crucial conversation, and I didn't want you coming over and disrupting it."

"Crucial?" Leo repeated, pointing at the chair across from him. "Ooh, have a seat. Do tell."

Clark plopped down and propped his elbows against the edge of the desk. "Long story short, Eva and I called a truce."

"Which one of you initiated that?"

"She did."

Snorting loudly, Leo rocked back in his chair. "And what made you agree to that? Your disastrous date from last night? Were you reminded of how good a woman Eva is? And forced to realize that it's time to get over the past and give her another—"

"Are you done?" Clark interrupted. "Because

if so, I can inform you that I'm taking Eva out tonight."

"Yes!" Leo shouted, pumping his fist in the air. "That's what I'm talking about, man! Get your girl back. Stop playing the field and settle down with the only woman you've ever loved."

"Hey, can you please calm down and lower your voice? You're getting ahead of yourself here. Tonight is not a date."

"Oh, really? What is it then?"

"Two people casually reconnecting. Eva is new in town, so I'm gonna show her around. That's all."

"Yeah, okay, *that's all,*" Leo rebutted, plunking back down in his chair. "I predict that you two will be back together before her temp assignment is over."

"Back together? When were we ever together in the first place?"

"You know what I mean. So, tell me, when are you gonna start deleting all those dating apps?"

As soon as the question escaped Leo's mouth, Clark's phone pinged with an alert from Two of Hearts.

"Do not say a word," he warned.

Leo responded with a throaty chuckle. "This is just too good. I wonder if that's Kelsie, wanting to talk about last night. Or maybe it's a new woman, reaching out to say hello. Why don't you pull out your phone and find out?"

Clark stood, waving him off. "I'm ignoring you. Anyway, my shift is over. It's time to head home and get ready for tonight."

"For your *date*?"

"For my *outing*. Have a nice evening, Director Graham."

On the way out the door, the hospital's intercom buzzed.

"Medical alert. Code Blue. First floor. Emergency Room."

Clark's phone buzzed with a text from Eva.

Code 99! Trauma victim with severe snakebites heading into the ER. Get here STAT!

"I've gotta go!" Clark told Leo before charging out of the office.

Clark shot through the ER and headed straight to the trauma unit.

"Which room?" he called out to the triage nurse.

"Ten!"

Clark caught a glimpse of a man wearing a Tarzan costume and a woman dressed as Jane hovering near the doorway. He brushed past them and hurried inside, diving right into the chaotic scene.

Paramedics had already transferred the patient from a stretcher onto the bed and disconnected the EMS monitor. Eva and Brandi were busy removing his bejeweled purple cape. Once they cut open his spandex bodysuit, several fang marks appeared on his neck, forearms, stomach and thighs. The wounds were red and swollen. Blood oozed from the puncture sites, while a few of them had already begun to blister.

"Rian?" Eva called out. "Where is that anti-venin?"

"Timothy went to grab it from the medication room! We keep it stored there inside the refrig-erator."

Clark washed his hands, threw on protective equipment and approached the bed. "Talk to me. What happened to our patient?"

"His name is Dexter," Eva said, "also known as the Poisonous Rattlesnake Tamer. According to his assistant, Dexter was bitten by at least three of the rattlesnakes he owns while practic-ing for their upcoming show."

"Did he specify which species?"

"A speckled rattlesnake, a sidewinder and a western diamondback."

"All pit vipers," Clark said. "Rian, does Tim-othy know that we need the polyvalent crotalid antivenin to neutralize the toxic effects of all three venoms?"

"He should, but I'll go check just to make sure," Rian responded before running out the door.

Clark bent down to get a better look at the wounds. "When did this attack occur?"

"Within the past hour," Brandi replied.

"Good. We're still within the first three hours of envenoming. That'll greatly increase our rate of success."

"Ahh..." Dexter moaned. His breathing appeared labored as his body began to convulse.

"Nurse Bennett," Eva said. "Cover his body with ice packs while I treat the wounds with glyceryl trinitrate ointment and pressure immobilization bandages. Dexter, this treatment is going to slow the spread of the venom until the antivenin starts working its magic, okay?"

"Oh—okay, but I… I'm so numb," he cried out. "And *hot*. I can't feel my legs." He pressed his thin, cracked lips together. *"Ew...* And my mouth tastes like rubber!"

"Those are all normal side effects after suffering a venomous snakebite," Clark told him just as Rian and Timothy returned. "Stay calm. We've got the antivenin here now, and it's a good one. The fragments of protein in it will work quickly to penetrate the tissue and offset the venom toxins. While I start the intravenous infusion, Dr. Gordon will continue treating your wounds while Nurse Bennett cools you down. Trust me, you're in good hands."

"I'm dizzy," Dexter moaned. "So dizzy. I can't see a thing. And I—I think I'm about to faint…"

"It's okay," Brandi said reassuringly while placing the ice packs against his chest. "These will help with the disorientation."

Eva moved toward one of the wounds on Dexter's thigh, brushing against Clark's body in the process. Her touch induced a sense of calm. Having her by his side filled a void that he hadn't realized was there.

Leaning into her, he asked, "What was Dexter's temperature last time you checked?"

"One hundred and three degrees. I gave him ibuprofen hoping it would reduce the fever along with any inflammation."

"Good. Rian, how is that antivenin IV setup coming along?"

"The line and bag are ready." He rolled the procedure tray toward Clark. "Which size needle would you like to use?"

"The sixteen gauge. Even though it's on the larger end of the spectrum, in a critical case like this, that size is necessary in order to get the antivenin flowing through the bloodstream as quickly as possible."

Clark wrapped a tourniquet around Dexter's right forearm, searched for a large, straight vein, then cleaned the area with an antiseptic swab. Once it was dry, he held the needle at a twenty-degree angle and inserted it, watching as a flashback of blood entered the flash chamber. After lowering the needle, he slid off the IV catheter.

"Do you need me to jump in over there?" Eva asked.

Clark tilted his head, watching as her fingers applied ointment meticulously over Dexter's bite marks. "No, I've got this covered. You're doing a great job treating those wounds."

"Thanks. I'm almost done. Has the infusion begun administering?"

"It has. The duration of this session will last for sixty minutes. Afterward, Dexter will need to remain under close observation for at least two hours. Do we have a dose of epinephrine close by?"

"Yes, it's on the procedure tray," Brandi responded.

"Do we have that in case of an allergic reaction to the antivenin?" Eva asked.

Clark nodded. "That's exactly right. In some cases, the antivenin can cause the patient's system to release a burst of chemicals that floods their bodies, which can lead to anaphylactic shock."

"So we should be on the lookout for a drop in blood pressure," Eva said while bandaging up the last bite mark. "Or swelling in the airway tissue that'll cause wheezing and shortness of breath, and of course loss of consciousness."

"You got it."

There was never a time when Eva wasn't impressive in a medical setting. But through the years they'd spent apart, she had blossomed into a remarkable physician. Clark was amazed by her ability to adapt to a hectic new environment in such a short amount of time.

"The patient's blood pressure is stable at one twenty-eight over eighty-seven," Eva said while studying the monitor.

"I see." Clark eyed the oximetry monitor clutching Dexter's right middle finger. "But his pulse is rising rapidly."

"Should we administer an adenosine injection or a diuretic?"

"Not yet. Let's allow the antivenin to go into effect. Once it does, his heart rate should decrease."

Brandi swooped in and held a straw to Dexter's lips. He drank the entire cup of ice water within seconds.

"Am I gonna live?" he rasped. "I've got a show scheduled for tomorrow. And there are several new moves the performers and I need to perfect. Where's Chuck? And Angel? And my snakes? *Where the hell are my snakes?*"

"Calm down, Dexter," Eva said, gently placing her hand on his arm. "Chuck and Angel are waiting for you in the lobby. Dr. Malone and I will check on them shortly and provide them with an update on your condition. Now, to answer your questions, yes, you're going to live. As for your snakes, I'm not sure where they are at this time, but I'm guessing your assistant may know. Once I find out I'll pass that information on to you. But in the meantime, I need for you to stay calm and allow the antivenin to take effect. Can you do that for me?"

"I'll try. Just make sure no one confiscated my snakes."

As Brandi took Dexter's temperature, Eva stepped back, joining Clark over by the mask and glove station.

He gave her a thumbs-up and a wink. "Great job, Doc. You're a pro at this. *All* of this. Have you ever considered doubling as a therapist? Because I love the way you just handled the patient."

With a shake of her head, she nudged his shoulder. "Absolutely not. I can barely manage the pace of this ER. After today, I might need therapy myself. Because seriously, I have never seen anything like this."

"In a city like Las Vegas, nothing surprises me anymore. This place is the capital of street performers. And everyone on the Strip is hustling to outdo the next act. Dexter isn't my first snake-taming bite victim, either. I've treated a few."

"Were you able to save them all?"

"I was, thankfully. We keep that antivenin fully stocked at all times. What these performers fail to realize is that their wild costars are not their friends. Especially venomous snakes. Those slithery creatures see tamers as nothing more than their next meal. Dexter's reptiles pumped that venom into his system for the sole purpose of paralyzing his body in preparation for digestion."

"That is chilling to say the least. I don't care how competitive it is out there. There's no way in hell I'm messing with those poisonous serpents."

"I hear that," Clark said before approaching Brandi. "What's his temperature now?"

"One hundred and one degrees. So it's going down."

"Good. Can you keep an eye on him while Eva and I go and talk to his partners?"

"Of course."

When Clark and Eva arrived in the waiting area, he overheard Chuck talking to Angel.

"Those snakes *love* Dexter," he sputtered as sweat trickled down his temples. "That much I know is true."

"But if they love him so much," Angel squeaked, "then why would they attack him?"

"Excuse us," Clark said, introducing himself and Eva.

"Doctors!" Chuck bellowed. "How is our boss? Is he alive? Is he gonna be okay?"

"He is alive," Clark said reassuringly, "and he's going to be okay. We're treating him with a very effective polyvalent crotalid antivenin.

It's working to neutralize the toxic effects of all three venoms in Dexter's system."

"Will he be discharged tonight?"

"No, not tonight. Considering the various venoms in his system, we'd like to observe him overnight. We'll have a better idea of when he'll be released in the morning."

"Well, when can we see him?" Angel asked.

"As soon as he's stable," Clark said. "Dr. Gordon and I will keep you posted on his condition."

Bowing in unison, Chuck and Angel lowered their heads. "We thank you, Doctors, for the glorious work that you've done," he proclaimed.

"You're very welcome," Clark replied before leading Eva back to the trauma unit. On the way there, she let off a deep yawn.

"Tired?" he asked, praying she wouldn't say yes and cancel their plans. While his focus had been on Dexter inside that operating room, the thought of spending an evening alone with Eva had lingered in the forefront of his mind. He couldn't wait to see her outside of the ER, wearing something way sexier than a pair of scrubs as they got caught up during their night out.

"I'm a little tired. I was heading out the door when Dexter was rushed into the ER. That was completely unexpected."

"It certainly was. Are you still up for our outing tonight, then maybe settling in somewhere quiet for dinner and drinks?"

Please say yes, Clark thought, his jaw tightening while awaiting her response.

"I don't know if I've got enough energy to explore the city after what we just went through."

The lump of anticipation pounding inside his chest fell to his feet.

"But I love the idea of a quiet dinner," Eva continued. "I'll tell you what. Why don't you come to my place later for wine and takeout? Nothing too fancy. Maybe Mexican? Or sushi?"

"Sushi would be perfect," Clark told her, his spirits immediately lifting.

"Great." She glanced at her watch. "Why don't we check back in with Dexter, complete patient handoffs, then go home to freshen up. Does eight o'clock work for you?"

"Most definitely."

"Okay then. Let's wrap up this day so we can get our night started."

CHAPTER SEVEN

"So how's working in a big city ER been compared to our cozy little clinic?" Amanda asked.

Eva clicked her tongue while digging around inside her makeup bag. "Let's see. It's been chaotic. Unpredictable. Shocking. Challenging. But more importantly, invaluable."

The friends were thirty minutes into a video chat as Eva prepared for her get-together with Clark, which Amanda kept insisting was a date.

"Oh," she continued, "and let's not forget extreme. You know what we're used to seeing in Black Willow. Patients with broken bones or shortness of breath. The occasional heart attack here and there. But in Las Vegas? I'm seeing a constant flow of patients suffering from drunken car accidents, stabbings, gunshot wounds, traumatic brain injuries...sometimes I feel like I'm struggling just to keep up."

"Well, considering where you are, I wouldn't expect much else. At least you've got Clark there for support. Speaking of which, how's it been working side by side with him again?"

"Good, actually. He's always very helpful and encouraging inside the ER. Outside of work, however, has been a different story. At least it was when I first got to town. He was pretty standoffish, more matter-of-fact than warm. Nothing like the guy we used to know. Med school Clark was kind and charming. Always buzzing with positive energy. But since I've been here, he's shown another side of himself. I honestly think he's still harboring some resentment toward me."

"I guess that's understandable. You did break the man's heart, Eva."

"I did," she admitted while applying a coat of mascara. "Anyway, Clark was much friendlier and more receptive toward me today. I'm hoping that means we're moving into a better place. And we'll stay there."

"Did he say anything about his date last night?"

"Nope, not really. When I asked about the rest of his evening, he was very dry. Didn't say much at all."

"So in other words, it was a bust." Amanda pulled the phone closer to her face, smirking mischievously into the camera. "Now back to you. Are you nervous about tonight?"

"*No*, I am not nervous. Why would I be?"

"Because you're about to spend some alone

time with the infamous Clark Malone! The man you should probably be married to by now. That's a pretty big deal. Plus, you seem a bit anxious. I can see your hands trembling all the way from Iowa. Breathe, friend, *breathe*."

Eva rolled her eyes until they strained while holding up two tubes of lip gloss. "Which of these shades do you like best? Sheer pink or orangey red?"

"Orangey red. It's sexier. It'll set off the vibes you're trying to give tonight."

"And what vibes are those, exactly?"

"The kind that scream you wanna take this thing between you and Clark outside of the ER and into the bedroom."

"Um…need I remind you that I'm still getting over being dumped by Kyle—"

"Kyle?" Amanda interrupted scathingly. "You mean the man who I warned you wasn't right for you? Who was never good enough for you?"

Swiping the orangey-red gloss across her lips, Eva uttered, "Look, don't make me hang up on you." It was all she could come up with considering Amanda was absolutely right. "And stop making this out to be more than what it is. I already told you that Clark is out here playing the field. He's not interested in starting up anything serious with me."

"Lies."

"No, *facts*. At best, he may want to rekindle our friendship. But that's it. He knows I'm only in Vegas for a few months. I highly doubt he'd want to be with someone who practically lives across the country. Not to mention Clark would probably never trust me with his heart again."

Responding with a frustrated groan, Amanda pressed her fingertips against her temples. "Eva, you and Clark are adults now. It sounds to me like he's trying to move forward and explore what could come of this situation. If that's the case, I hope you'll open yourself up to the idea."

Eva hopped up and assessed herself in the mirror, smoothing her black halter dress over her hips. "I'm ignoring you. Now, are you sure this outfit looks okay?"

"It looks perfect. *You* look perfect. The soft beach waves cascading over your shoulders, the subtle makeup with a pop of color on the lips. It's all working for you, girl. So, tell me again, what's on this evening's agenda?"

"Nothing too fancy. Since Clark and I were too tired to go out and explore the city, I invited him over for wine and sushi."

"Humph. Sounds like a pretty intimate evening to me."

"It's just two people unwinding and catching up over a meal, Amanda."

A series of bells chimed from Eva's phone.

Clark had texted.

On my way. Stopping off to pick something up first. See you soon…

She jumped when Amanda tapped loudly on the screen. "What's with the huge grin plastered across your face? Was that a message from your man?"

"It was a message from *Clark*, letting me know he's on his way."

"Okay, well, before you go, I'd just like to say that I am so glad you two have finally buried the hatchet and started anew. You're working well together, and now I'm hoping you'll start playing well together, too."

"And on that note, I'm hanging up. Have a nice evening, Dr. Reinhart."

"Call me as soon as you can! I wanna hear all about the sexy little romp that's about to take—"

Eva disconnected the chat. The nerves churning inside her stomach wouldn't allow for jokes, let alone thoughts of sleeping with Clark.

She busied herself around the apartment until her phone pinged, alerting her that a guest was in the lobby. After allowing Clark entry, Eva took one last look in the mirror, then waited by the door. Her beating heart thumped inside her eardrums.

Deep breath in, deep breath out...

The elevator dinged. She peered through the peephole, squeezing the door handle for dear life.

Tonight is going to be a good night. Just keep it light. Casual. Friendly.

Eva jolted when Clark knocked. "Hi!" she exclaimed much louder than intended after flinging open the door.

"Hey," he murmured through an amused grin.

She stepped aside and let him in, anxious for a glass of wine.

Seductive notes of bergamot and sandalwood followed Clark inside. By the looks of his freshly cut hair and perfectly trimmed goatee, he'd just left the barbershop. He appeared cool on the surface. But there was a buzz of energy in his steps, as if there was no place he'd rather be than there with her.

"This place is really nice," he said, scanning the apartment.

"Thanks. I've spent the majority of my free time trying to make it feel like home."

He strolled through the living room, pausing at the framed photos of her family and friends lining the fireplace mantel. "I see several familiar faces here. Aren't some of these the same photographs you had at your apartment during med school?"

"They are. Good memory."

"Those days are hard to forget."

A swirl of tension rushed through Eva's chest. She wondered if there was an underlying meaning behind his statement, as if he wanted more of what they'd once shared.

He leaned forward, crossing his arms while studying a black-and-white photo of Eva and Amanda. His biceps flexed through the sleeves of his cream cashmere sweater. Her eyes wandered down to his slim-cut gray slacks. The bulge in front sent her mind wandering down paths that were far from friendly.

Do not go there...

"What is that in your hand?" Eva asked, pointing at the bakery box in his hand.

"A little sweet treat for after dinner. And you won't believe what it is."

She followed Clark into the kitchen, slightly turned on by the way he'd made himself at home. He set the package on the white marble countertop and lifted the lid.

"Smell that?" he asked. "Can you guess what it is yet?"

The scent of vanilla and coconut drifted from the box.

"You didn't."

"Oh, but I did."

She peered down at the Louisiana crunch cake, touched that he remembered her obsession with Entenmann's version back when they were in school. Giving his arm a squeeze, Eva said, "Your memory really is impeccable, you know that? I mean, is there *anything* that you've forgotten?"

"When it comes to you? Not really, no."

The words lingered in the air as the pair fell silent. Clark took a step closer, his hand brushing against hers when he reached for a glass. "May I?"

She slid a bottle of sauvignon blanc toward him. "Yes, please. Thank you."

While he poured the wine Eva plated the sushi, fighting to steady her shaky hands.

"Ooh, you ordered from Kaiseki Yuzu?" Clark asked. "Good choice."

"Brandi told me about it. You should've seen the look on her face when I told her we were hanging out tonight."

"If it was anything like the one on Leo's when I told him, I already know."

A wavering chuckle slipped through Eva's lips. "Those two…always insinuating something that isn't even there. You may as well throw Amanda into the mix, too. She's just as bad, if not worse."

"Really? I'm curious to know what she had to say about this unexpected reunion."

"You know Amanda. She's into the whole cosmic alignment, synchronicity, spiritual woo-woo thing. So…"

"So she thinks fate brought us back together?"

"Exactly."

Clark handed her a glass of wine. "What do you think?"

Eva took a long sip before responding. "I think it's always nice to reconnect with an old friend…"

His penetrating stare sent a rush of heat through her body. Eva turned away, leaning into the counter while sliding sashimi onto a plate.

"What else do we have here?" Clark asked, peering into one of the takeout containers. "I see a little bit of everything."

"I think I ordered the entire menu. We've got tofu, black edamame, mixed tempura, grilled eel, nigiri…"

"Mmm, sounds delish…" He hesitated when his phone pinged. "Excuse me one sec."

Don't look, Eva told herself.

But her eyes defied her as they wandered toward the screen. A double heart logo appeared next to a text box. It was the same logo she'd seen when his date texted him at the Oasis.

Eva cringed against the pull in her chest. She took a long sip of wine, hoping it would wash down the jealousy burning her throat.

A look of irritation crossed his face. He shoved the cell back in his pocket without opening the message.

"Shall we?" he asked, carrying their plates to the dining room table.

"Yes, please." She grabbed their glasses and smiled, that twinge dissipating as she followed him.

"I'm so glad we're doing this," Clark said. "I needed it. *We* needed it. A nice, chill night after a super hectic day inside the ER."

"I concur. Working in Fremont General's emergency room is more than a notion."

"It is. But you've adjusted to it extremely well."

"Thank you," Eva said through a soft smile. "Having you there with me has been a huge help. I'm still getting used to it, though. I'm sure I'll settle in eventually."

"In my opinion, you already have. You were a highly skilled leader when you arrived. Now you continue to show that leadership with every patient you treat.

"And the same goes for you. You've really grown as a physician, Clark. And you have certainly become a great doctor."

"Thanks, E. I take that as a high compliment, coming from you." He paused, his eyes roaming her body. "Did I mention how good you look tonight?"

"Okay, *that* came out of nowhere," Eva retorted, taken aback by his flattery as she hid her flaming cheeks behind a napkin. "But no, you didn't."

"Well, you do."

"Thank you."

"You're welcome."

The fire in his stare sent her scrambling for a new subject. "So, tell me, how's life been since you left the Midwest for the West Coast?"

"It's been good. For starters, I love the weather. Growing up in Chicago, then going to Michigan for college and Iowa for med school, meant icy-cold winters filled with a ton of snow. Then I move out here, and we're talking balmy days, pleasant nights, barely any rain. It is heaven. And don't even get me started on the scenery. The mountains, the palm trees…it's unreal."

"What about the women? Have you noticed any distinct differences there?"

"Uh-oh," Clark murmured after sliding an edamame pod between his lips. "Why do I have a feeling you're about to grill me about my personal life?"

"Because I am."

"Ha! So, it's only fair that I turn the heat up on you too then, right?"

Eva shrugged, swallowing a slice of salmon. "Of course. But if we're going there, then let me ask you this. Why are you still single?"

"Ooh, now you're pulling out the heavy artillery! I'm gonna need more wine for this." After taking a long sip, he said, "Seriously though, the answer to that question is simple. I haven't been able to settle down with the one."

Brandi's words about being Clark's "one that got away" sprang to Eva's mind.

She'd brushed it off before, but excitement stirred as she wondered whether there was some truth to those words after all.

"Not to mention I've just been focusing on work since moving out here," he continued. "You know how hectic this job is. And these days, since my professional life is such a priority, I keep the whole dating thing casual. That way I can remain at the top of my game with no distractions. It's a win-win situation if you ask me."

Eva held her breath, waiting for him to make a snarky comment about how she could probably relate to his mentality. Surprisingly, he didn't.

There was something cold about his statement, empty even, that made her wonder if this was how he'd felt back in the day when she had prioritized her studies over him and their friendship—especially after their steamy night together.

But what really struck Eva yet again was how much he'd changed. Clark had never been one to push love away. He'd always thrived on relationships and creating meaningful bonds. A hint of sadness hit as she couldn't help feeling somewhat responsible for his attitude now.

"What about you?" he asked, refilling their glasses. "What went down between you and your ex, if I may ask?"

The question stiffened her back. It was only

right that she answer him considering how open he'd been with her. "Where do I even start?"

"Wherever you're most comfortable."

"Well, just to give you a little background info, Kyle and I met at a charity event and dated for five years."

"Five years? That's a long time."

"Yeah, it is. Funny how we invested so much time into something that ended so abruptly. But anyway, he proposed a little over a year ago, and the moment I said yes, both of our mothers immediately started planning the wedding. I admit I got wrapped up in the whirlwind of it all, too, and before I knew it, our nuptials became the talk of Black Willow. We were both under a lot of pressure. And stress. Not to mention drama. Kyle is running for state senator, and he's in the middle of a heated campaign. The wedding planning got to be too much for him, so he broke things off."

"Just like that?"

"Just like that."

"*Wow*. I'm sorry you had to go through that," Clark said, reaching across the table and clutching her hand. "It couldn't have been easy, especially if you were in love."

His comment should have been a statement. But it sounded more like a question.

Eva held her fist to her chin. "You know, it's interesting you should say that. Because after the breakup, I was forced to reassess the relationship and face whether or not Kyle and I were ever *really* in love. Was what we had real? Or did the relationship simply look good on paper? Does that make sense?"

"That makes perfect sense. Just because two people *should* be good together doesn't mean they actually are. A prominent doctor and a potential senator sound like a great pairing, right?"

"Exactly. But were we really? I don't think so. Because underneath it all, I've come to realize there wasn't ever any real passion between Kyle and me. Were we content? Yes. *Happy?* I thought so. Maybe I'd mistaken comfort for happiness. I'd convinced myself that the respect we'd garnered from the Black Willow community was enough to sustain us. And admittedly, I'd gotten caught up in being the quintessential power couple. That made up for the fact that there was no spark. No thrill. And actually, no real affection between us, not like there had been between—"

You and me, she almost let slip.

"So basically," Clark said after a pause, "you two were more like colleagues than lovers."

"Pretty much."

After popping the last piece of hosomaki in his mouth, Clark picked up their plates and stood. "Well, good riddance to him. No matter what you and I may have been through in the past, I've always known that you're an amazing woman,

Eva. You deserve more than a partner who only looks good on paper. You deserve it all."

"Thank you for saying that, Clark."

She followed him into the kitchen, almost stumbling over the plethora of emotions stirring through her limbs. The moment was reminiscent of the evening they'd slept together all those years ago. Just like tonight, the combination of alcohol, good conversation and undeniable attraction had gone straight to her head. Eva could feel the promise she'd made to herself to keep things professional draining from her body.

"How about we finish off this bottle of wine over on the couch?" she suggested.

"You must've been reading my mind. I'd love to stretch out. Give these sore muscles a rest. Are you ready for a slice of this cake?"

"Absolutely." She pulled a couple of dessert plates down and handed Clark a knife. Instead of cutting two pieces, he cut one and fed a sliver to her.

"Mmm, this is delicious."

"I knew you'd love it. Melts right in your mouth, doesn't it?"

"It does."

He fed her another piece. This time, his fingers lingered on her lips. Eva moved closer, their bodies inches apart. Clark tilted her chin and searched her eyes, looking for a hint of permission. She nodded, leaning in as their lips parted.

His tongue slipped between hers, swirling softly, then retreating, then going back for more.

Eva felt him harden against her thigh. Spreading her knees apart, he grabbed her by the hips and lifted her onto the island. Their mouths melted into each other's as he thrust his pelvis between her legs. She moaned, falling back while his teeth pulled at her neckline. They nibbled her breasts and teased her taut nipples. His fingertips clawed at her panties while she ripped open his zipper. Before she could wrap her hands around him, Clark dropped to his knees and buried his face between her thighs.

Eva's entire body stiffened, then trembled as her hips moved to the rhythm of his tongue, then his fingers, then his tongue once again. She shivered, emitting a scream almost loud enough to awaken the entire block.

"Looks like you found that spark you've been missing," he grunted in her ear. "Because you just exploded inside my mouth."

Before she could respond, Clark lifted her off the island and carried her into the bedroom. Their clothes were off within seconds. Eva wrapped her legs around his waist as his hands explored every inch of her body, from the edge of her earlobes to the soles of her feet.

Despite only being together that one time way back when, Clark's insatiable touch still felt familiar. His scent, a mix of fresh perspiration and musky cologne, still awakened her senses. And his tongue, assertive and commanding, still made her quiver.

But this was more than just a physical connection. Clark's body evoked deep emotional memories from their past. The long talks and shared secrets that formed a bond she'd thought was unbreakable. Once it dissolved, Eva assumed it was gone forever. Yet here they were, reconnecting in the most intimate way. It was as thrilling as it was scary. Because considering her vulnerable state and their tumultuous history, she feared this dangerous territory could lead to irreparable pain.

In this moment, however, as Clark bit into her neck, Eva swallowed the regret she felt for ever letting him go. The signs of him being the type of man she'd always wanted were all there. Still. And when he plunged deep inside her, she questioned whether she could let him go again once her time in Vegas was up. That's if he'd even want her to stay...

CHAPTER EIGHT

CLARK AWAKENED TO the blaring chirp of an alarm. His eyes shot open and darted around the room. After a few moments, he realized that he was still at Eva's, inside her bedroom.

Surreal...

His head gradually rose from the pillow. She was resting comfortably on his chest, her wavy hair cascading down the side of her face. Even in a deep sleep, she still managed to look beautiful.

Clark reached over and tapped the snooze button on her phone. It was only 5:45 a.m. Another fifteen minutes of sleep wouldn't hurt. They weren't due back at the hospital until eight.

What in the hell are you doing? You don't ever spend the night at women's apartments. Get up and go home!

But this wasn't just any woman. This was Eva Gordon. For her, he could make an exception. At least this one time...

She stirred slightly, her supple lips forming a soft smile. Although her eyes were still closed, her hand managed to find his erection. Clark groaned, watching as her head skimmed his chest, his stomach, then disappeared underneath the sheet.

Eva took him inside her mouth, her jaws tightening as she devoured his entire shaft.

Every muscle in his body tensed. He gripped the side of the bed, thinking *Don't you dare...* when the tip slid past the back of her throat. *Hold it. Hold it!*

"I can't do this," Clark muttered, unable to control the tremors in his legs as he struggled to hold back his orgasm. "I'm not ready yet..."

Despite his body throbbing to release, he threw off the sheet and pulled Eva up by the shoulders. She fell on top of him, hungrily covering his mouth with hers while straddling him with ease. His moans vibrated against her tongue as she arched her back and guided him inside. Their bodies thrust in unison, grinding to the beat of their own familiar rhythm.

Within minutes, they climaxed together. Eva collapsed onto Clark's chest, heaving as he stared up at the ceiling in utter disbelief.

"Well," he panted, "*that* was completely unexpected."

"Yes, it was. Both last night and this morning."

"True. How in the hell did we just go from zero to a hundred like that? I mean, one minute we were having a little dessert, and then the next minute…"

"We were on top of the kitchen island," Eva murmured, grazing his forearm with her fingertips. "I have no idea. But in all honesty? I loved every minute of it."

"So did I."

Silence fell over the pair. But Clark's emotions were far from settled. His feelings for Eva had never left. Over the years, he'd managed to bury them. Last night, however, he'd realized not only had they resurfaced, but they'd come back with a vengeance.

Pull back. Don't forget that Eva is on the rebound and on borrowed time. Three months from now she'll be back in Black Willow, repairing the life she abandoned. Don't set yourself up for failure again.

The reminder was all Clark needed to hit the internal reset button. He rolled over, grabbed his cell and slid toward the edge of the bed.

"I was thinking I could put on a pot of coffee," Eva said. "Scramble some eggs, toast a couple of bagels—"

"I actually need to get going," he interrupted. "I have a few errands to run before work."

The lie was out of his mouth before he knew it. But he'd had to come up with something to release the fear tightening his chest. If Clark left fast enough, he wouldn't have to hear Eva tell him that this was just a onetime thing, and they shouldn't mix business with pleasure. It was his way of getting in front of the situation before it imploded in his face.

"Hey," Eva said, grabbing his hand. "Before you go, are we going to, um…talk about all this?"

"'This' meaning…?" Clark probed, quickly hopping into his gray boxer briefs.

Anxiety simmered in his gut, igniting memories of that night they'd spent together during med school. The elation he'd felt, thinking he and Eva would finally be together. It was indescribable. So was the devastation he'd felt after she'd rejected him.

"'This' meaning us," Eva continued, sitting straight up. "What happened between you and me last night. And this morning."

Don't bite. Keep the ball in her court. See where she takes it.

"It was amazing," Clark told her while pulling on his pants. "Did you enjoy yourself?"

"Of course. Which begs the question, where do we go from here?"

"Where do you want to go from here?"

She turned toward the window, staring out at the palm leaves blowing in the wind. "That's a pretty complicated question," Eva said before pulling off the sheet and revealing her toned, naked body.

Thoughts of lying beside her, being inside her

while kissing those soft lips and lush breasts, caused Clark to harden against his zipper. He looked away, resisting the urge to throw her back down onto the bed and indulge in a third round of lovemaking.

Eva stood, slipping on a cream satin robe, then pulling her hair into a low bun. "I know that you're casually dating or whatever. I'm fresh off a breakup and only in Las Vegas for a short while…"

Here we go. This is the part where she tells me this was fun, but that we should consider it a one and done.

"But honestly?" she continued, sauntering over and running her hands along his shoulder blades. "I still have feelings for you, Clark."

Wait…what?

She stood on her tippy-toes, teasing his lips with her tongue.

"So what are you saying?" he asked in between kisses.

"What I'm saying is I want to continue whatever this is we've started. I don't know exactly what that means, or what it'll look like. But what I do know is I want to explore the idea of us being together, in some capacity."

Clark didn't quite know how to respond. So he remained silent, opting to keep his lips glued to hers until he could think things through.

Being with Eva felt good. And right. It was

what he'd always wanted. But the pain she'd caused in the past ran deep. He'd managed to heal and was in a good place. Putting his heart on the line once more at the risk of being hurt again did not seem like a good idea. Clark knew he may never recover from losing her a second time.

"Well?" Eva asked, her hands gently cradling the sides of his face. "What do you think?"

He glanced down, mesmerized by her hopeful gaze.

"I'm in," he blurted out.

What are you doing?

"You are?" she exclaimed.

At least protect yourself by putting some stipulations on it!

"I am. But I think we need to lay some ground rules."

Eva's arms fell by her sides.

"Ground rules? What do you mean?"

"What I mean is, you've got a lot going on, and so do I. If we want to establish an intimate relationship, then I think we should keep things casual. No expectations, and no catching feelings. Most importantly, our hooking up cannot interfere with work."

Judging by the dimming spark in her eyes, Eva wasn't too keen on the idea. Clark hoped he hadn't turned her off. But for him, there was no room for error. While both she and his high school sweetheart had broken his heart, it was the relationship with Eva that he mourned the most. Eva was special. A best friend, classmate and confidante that he'd truly grown to love. Their demise had left a gaping hole in his heart that had never been filled. This time around he had to put his needs first. Back in the day she'd held all the power. It was his turn now to reconnect on a deeper level while holding back on the emotions. Because when it came down to it, Clark still didn't trust that Eva would keep his heart intact.

"So you and I will continue to see each other with no strings attached," Eva responded slowly. "Is that what you want?"

"That's exactly what I want. You do your thing, I'll do mine, and we'll come together whenever we want. *Literally.* We wouldn't be exclusive, so if we choose to hang out with other people, we can. And I also think we should keep this between us. I don't want our situation-ship to interfere with work and draw unwanted attention from our colleagues."

"Oh, please. You know you're gonna tell Leo. He's your best friend."

Glancing down at his phone, Clark chuckled then showed her the screen. "I've already got two missed calls and three texts from him this morning. Trust me, he's already making assumptions.

But anyway, back to us. What do you think of my proposition?"

"What I'm thinking is," she whispered, leading him back toward the bed, "I'm in."

"Good," he moaned, pulling off her robe on the way there.

CHAPTER NINE

EVA STROLLED THROUGH the door of Fremont General's physician's lounge, unable to turn down the grin on her face.

"Good morning, everyone!" she crooned to several doctors she'd never seen before. They nodded, mumbling an inaudible greeting before turning back to their conversations.

Calm down. Everyone here isn't matching your energy.

Every cell in her body was buzzing. It was a feeling she hadn't experienced in a long time, if ever. Gone were the pangs of anxiety plaguing her mind whenever she'd arrive at the hospital, anticipating what the day would bring. They'd been replaced by a sense of calm mingled with excitement. Apparently, hooking up with Clark had been exactly what she'd needed to settle into a new city.

That's what Eva's mind said. But her heart was thumping to the tune of a different emotion. She'd been caught off guard when Clark suggested they keep things casual. As presumptuous as it may have been, Eva thought he'd be all in and want way more. She could feel herself slipping in that direction, too.

But the idea alone sparked a sharp reminder of what she'd just gone through with Kyle. The pain of giving five years of her life to a man who didn't deserve her love and loyalty was something she didn't want to relive. So maybe it was a good thing that Clark only wanted a fling. A casual affair would force Eva to keep her emotions in check while adding some spice to her three-month stint in Las Vegas.

Regardless of the box Clark had squeezed their relationship into, she felt good about the reunion. Eva would enjoy it for what it was, rack up all the knowledge she could working inside Fremont General's ER, then return to Black Willow with the hope that they'd remain friends.

Pressure filled Eva's head at the thought of going back home. While she hadn't been in Las Vegas long, the city had already grown on her. Especially after last night. Would leaving really be that easy?

The good news is you don't have to worry about it right now. So don't.

Eva poured herself a cup of coffee and exited the lounge, running into Brandi as she rounded the corner.

"Good morning, Eva!"

"Good morning, Brandi. How are you?"

"Exhausted. I stayed here pretty late last night so I could keep an eye on our snakebite victim. I knew he was in good hands with Dr. Abrams, but I just couldn't leave his side. I mean, all those bites from three different snakes? I'd never seen anything like it."

"How is Dexter doing?"

"Really well. He was released early this morning. But Dr. Abrams told him to come back to the ER if he experiences any excessive pain, swelling or shortness of breath."

"Good. I hope he abides by that. What treatment plan did the doctor send him home with?"

Brandi extended her right hand, ticking off her fingers as she spoke. "Prescriptions for ibuprofen, ampicillin, a topical antiseptic and glyceryl trinitrate ointment. I spoke with Dexter's assistants, who stayed in the waiting area all night, and they're going to manage his care at home. Seems like he'll be in good hands. On a side note, the work that you and Clark did to keep Dexter alive was outstanding. Dr. Abrams was amazed that he wasn't in much worse shape."

"Thank you. You did a tremendous job as well. That was actually my first time treating a snakebite victim, so I can't take too much credit. Clark did most of the heavy lifting."

"I love your humility, Eva, but I'd say it was fifty-fifty. Speaking of Clark…"

Here we go.

"Did you two have a good time last night?"

"We did. Clark and I had originally made plans to go out and explore the city. But after treating Dexter, we were both exhausted. So he came to my place for dinner and drinks."

The mere mention of their evening prompted a burst of flashbacks. Clark's fingers, caressing her lips as he fed her cake. His tongue, massaging her nipples. Their bodies, shuddering together while he—

"Eva?"

"Oh, I'm sorry. What were you saying?"

The smirk on Brandi's face told Eva everything she needed to know. The nurse knew she had Clark on the brain.

While Eva had grown quite fond of Brandi and was dying to discuss her evening, she didn't want to break her promise to Clark.

"I was saying that I'm glad you're creating a life outside of the hospital," Brandi continued. "Making friends in a city like Las Vegas can be hard. And even though you'll only be here for three months, it's nice that you've already developed a little friendship circle."

"Thanks. So am I. Having you, Clark and Leo around has really helped me settle in and feel welcome."

Loud voices boomed through the air as the ER doors swung open. Snapping into work mode,

Eva said, "Sounds like the emergency room is packed with patients."

"Surprisingly, it's not. A good number of patients were transferred to different units last night and early this morning. But who knows what the day will bring. Dr. Abrams has already done the handoff with Clark, so he'll bring you up to speed on everyone's current conditions."

"Oh, Clark is already here?"

"Yes. He arrived about forty-five minutes ago."

Eva's stomach flipped as they entered the emergency room.

"The situation definitely had its challenges," she heard behind her. "But thank goodness the patient pulled through."

Peeking over her shoulder, Eva saw Clark standing near the front desk speaking to a pretty young medical assistant.

"Yes, thanks to *you*, Dr. Malone," the woman purred, pulling her fingers through a fake blond ponytail. "All that venom rushing through your poor patient's bloodstream? He could have died!"

"He could've. But luckily, he didn't. I'm just grateful I had such a great team working with me. Dr. Gordon in particular. Speaking of which," he said after noticing Eva.

Hearing him mention her name almost sent Eva's feet levitating off the speckled tile floor. She waved, watching as he excused himself, then sauntered over. There was a glint in Clark's stare that held their little secret. The corners of his lips curled slightly, as if suppressing a smile.

"Good morning, Dr. Gordon. Nurse Bennett."

"Good morning, Doc," Brandi chirped. "Are you done with the handoff?"

"I am." His gaze shifted from her to Eva. That grin he'd been fighting to detain came bursting through, his gleaming white teeth lighting up the entire waiting area. "And I'm ready to get Dr. Gordon all caught up on our roster of patients."

Silence fell over the group. Eva knew it was her turn to respond. But she'd fallen into some sort of trance, staring at Clark's handsome face as if they were the only two people there. The charts he shuffled in his hands evoked thoughts of his fingers gripping her back. His lips, as he spoke, were just immersed in between her thighs a few hours ago. That tongue was—

"Dr. Gordon?" Brandi said. *"Dr. Gordon!"*

Eva's neck whipped in her direction. "Um… I…yes? Were you saying something?"

"I was asking if you need anything before I go restock the patients' rooms with extra linens."

Gently nudging her shoulder, Clark asked, "What's going on with you, Dr. Gordon? Long night?"

She swallowed the snicker climbing her throat. "I actually slept very well last night. Thank you."

"That wasn't my question."

Will you stop that? Eva's wide-eyed expression screamed.

Ignoring Clark's satisfied smirk, she turned to Brandi. "I think I'm all set. Go ahead and take care of the rooms while I review the patient charts with Dr. Malone. I'll check back in with you afterward."

"Okay…" Brandi slowly nodded while backing away, her arched eyebrows furrowing into her crinkled forehead.

"Somebody knows what we did last night…" Clark whispered in Eva's ear.

"Clark!" she protested. "Would you please cut it out? Weren't you the one who was so insistent on us keeping this little…*whatever* it is we're doing, away from work?"

"I was. And I have yet to break that rule. So what are you even talking about?"

"Oh, okay. Now you wanna play innocent—"

Eva stopped when the sound of pounding footsteps approached from behind.

"Hey!" Leo called out, barreling toward them. "Just the people I need to see. Brandi, get back over here. I'm in a bind. And I need you. All three of you."

"What's going on?" Clark asked.

"Rita is hosting a huge charity gala for Yvonne's House. It's just over three weeks from now, and you all have to be there."

"Wait, who's Rita?" Eva asked.

"Leo's ex-wife," Clark told her.

"Oh…" she breathed, surprised to hear that Leo had been married. "And, please forgive me for not knowing, but what exactly is Yvonne's House?"

"A nonprofit organization that advocates for the homeless here in Las Vegas," Brandi replied. "Rita is the head of the board."

Leo, who was now sweating profusely, threw his hands on top of his shiny head and pivoted in frustration. "I was dumb enough to tell her that I'd attend the event. I mean, of course I wanna support the cause and all, so when she asked, I couldn't just say no."

"Understood," Clark said. "You're definitely doing the right thing by going. But am I missing something here? Why don't you want to go anymore?"

"Better yet," Brandi chimed in, "why do you need for us to go, too? I'm all for supporting the organization as well, but it sounds like there's more to this than just purchasing a ticket."

"There is," Leo panted. "First of all, Clark, to answer your question, the reason why I don't wanna go anymore is because I just found out Rita is seeing someone, and she's bringing him as her date! Secondly, to answer *your* question, Brandi, I need you all there for moral support.

I am *not* ready to see my ex-wife on the arm of another man."

"Wait a minute," Clark interjected. "According to you, there was no love lost after the divorce and you've never wanted Rita back."

"There wasn't. And I don't."

"So why would you care if she brings another man to the gala?"

"Look, just because I don't want to *be* with Rita doesn't mean I wanna see her with somebody else!" Leo turned on his heels and muttered to Brandi, "Which brings me to my next question…"

"Why do I get the feeling you're about to say something outrageous?"

"Because I am. Bran," he began, crouching as though he was going down on one knee before thinking twice and standing back up. "Would you please, *please* attend the event as my date?"

"As your *what*?"

"As my date! I mean, not my *real* date. Just like a fake date. Because there is no way in hell I'm stepping foot inside of Château Le Jardin's banquet hall alone."

An awkward silence fell over the group. All eyes were on Brandi as she dropped her head into her hand. "Let me get this straight. You want me to pretend that I'm your date, and act like we're a…a real couple?"

"Exactly."

Giving her a reassuring pat on the arm, Eva said, "Come on, Brandi. I think it's a cute idea. Plus, you and Leo always have a great time together. Just pretend like it's a night out at the Oasis rather than a fake dating scenario. Clark and I will be right there with you, won't we, Clark?"

"We absolutely will. I'm all in."

"See?" Eva told Brandi. "It'll be fun. Not to mention you'd be doing your good friend a huge favor."

Leo pointed his praying hands in Eva's direction. "Thank you for your vote of confidence, Eva."

"Don't mention it. I'm team Leo, all the way."

While Eva had meant every word she'd said, it was the thrill of spending an evening out with Clark that swayed her the most. Feeling his gaze on her, she glanced over, grinning when he mouthed the words, *You're the best.*

"So?" Leo asked Brandi. "What do you think?"

She threw her head back and stared up at the ceiling. "What's the dress code?"

"Black tie. Does that question mean you're actually considering it?"

"Maybe…"

As Leo's expression brightened with hope, Eva turned to Brandi. "You know what that means?

We'll have to go dress shopping. I didn't pack any formal attire. That would be fun, wouldn't it?"

"It would."

"Pretty please," Leo crooned, his feet now shuffling from side to side.

"All right, fine," Brandi sighed. "I'll go. But you're gonna owe me for this one, buddy. *Big* time."

He grabbed her by the waist and swung her around. "Anything you want, I'll do it. Anything!"

"The first thing you can do is calm down!"

As they continued bantering back and forth, Clark sidled up next to Eva.

"Well, it looks like we've got our first formal outing here in Las Vegas on the books."

"Looks like we do."

"What kind of dress are you thinking of wearing?"

"I don't know. What kind of dress would you like to see me in?"

"Something sexy, for sure."

Exaggerated throat-clearing interrupted the conversation. Eva and Clark swiveled, realizing that Leo and Brandi were watching them.

"What is this I'm seeing here?" Leo asked. "You two are up to something, aren't you? What's going on?"

"Nothing!" they declared in unison.

"A-actually," Eva stammered, "we were just talking about the charity event."

"Yeah, and…discussing what Eva is planning to wear."

"Why would you be concerned with what she's planning to—"

"Leo," Brandi interrupted, "why don't you walk with me while I head back to the patients' rooms? You can check on them and make sure they don't need anything or have any issues."

Before he could respond, she pulled him away while giving Eva a sly wink.

"I think we'd better tone it down at work," Eva warned Clark.

"We should. But considering all the things you did to my body last night and this morning, that's gonna be hard."

"For the sake of our jobs, try harder," she said as they started down the hallway.

"Yes, Doctor."

Just as Eva reached for his stack of patient charts, Clark grabbed her by the waist and pulled her inside a supply closet.

"Hey!" she gasped. "What are you doing?" Not that she cared. For once in her life, Eva was less concerned with work and more into the moment with Clark.

He responded by pressing his lips against hers.

"You're not even trying," Eva murmured in between deep, lingering kisses.

Clark thrust his groin against her thigh. "Not at all."

"You almost popped open a button on my lab coat."

"That's not all I'm trying to pop open. I need to see you again. Outside of here."

"And you will. But in the meantime, we'd better get back to work before both of us get fired."

"You're right," he huffed, readjusting his pants before opening the door. "After you."

Eva peeked down the hallway, making sure the coast was clear while wishing she'd brought a change of underwear. When Clark grabbed her backside on the way out, she moaned, now eager to get that hookup on the calendar sooner rather than later.

CHAPTER TEN

EVA CLIMBED THE stairs to Clark's condo, excited for the night ahead. They'd had a wonderful morning and afternoon exploring Las Vegas, from a visit to the Mob Museum and Hoover Dam Bypass to the Mandalay Bay Shark Reef and fried chicken burgers at CRAFTkitchen. In between destinations Clark had acted as her personal tour guide, showing her the various sights along the way.

After going home to shower and change, they were now heading to Restaurant Guy Savoy at Caesars Palace for fine French cuisine. Eva had already checked out the menu and couldn't decide on which decadent meal to indulge in. The Dungeness crab and Kusshi oysters, Wagyu filet and smoked potatoes, Muscovy duck breast and smoked duck sausage all looked delectable. She'd settled on allowing Clark to choose.

Eva had volunteered to get behind the wheel for their night out since he'd been driving all day. She rang the bell and headed back to her rented silver Audi Q3. Instead of coming downstairs, he buzzed the door.

"Now why wouldn't you just meet me outside?" she muttered.

Eva ran back up and grabbed the handle before the main door locked, then knocked on his condo door. Her fist pushed it open.

"Clark?" she called out.

There was no answer.

Confusion hit as Eva stuck her head inside. The lights were turned down so low that she could barely see. Once her eyes adjusted to the darkness, she noticed soft candlelight flickering throughout the living room.

She stepped inside. Vases filled with red roses were propped in each corner. A bottle of wine was chilling inside a bucket on top of the kitchen's quartz countertop. But Clark was nowhere in sight.

"What is all this?" Eva murmured right before a warm body pressed against her backside.

"What took you so long to get here?" Clark whispered, wrapping her up in his arms.

"One of my neighbors stopped me on the way out and asked a ton of questions about how to treat his recurring dyshidrosis eczema."

"Interesting. Were you able to help him?"

"I was. I recommended a trip to the dermatologist, oral and topical steroids, and drainage for the larger, more painful blisters." She spun around within his grasp. "Um…what is going on here?"

"Did I mention how beautiful you look?" Clark asked, ignoring her question. "And are you hungry?"

Eva straightened the hem on her one-shoulder satin minidress. "You didn't, but thank you. And, yes. I'm starving. Are we still going out to dinner, or—" She hesitated, inhaling the delicious aroma floating through the air. "Wait, are you cooking?"

"I am. We've had a long day. I figured that a nice, intimate meal at my place would be better than fighting our way through all the tourists on the Strip. Wouldn't you agree?"

Slowly nodding, Eva took another look around the condo. "I would. So, wait, was all this pre-arranged?"

"Somewhat. It was a bit last-minute, but I think I pulled it off. Do you like it?"

"I love it."

Taking her hand in his, Clark led Eva to the dining area. "Good. And don't worry. I promise I'll take you to Guy Savoy's another time. Tonight, I just want you all to myself."

"Well, you got me," she told him, her body heating up in anticipation.

Clark's oval glass table was adorned with tall tapered candles, blue porcelain dinnerware and crystal wineglasses.

"Have a seat," he said, pulling out a chair. "I'll be right back."

Eva sat gingerly, taking it all in. Everything was so thoughtful. And romantic. And far beyond what anyone would do for a casual hookup buddy. The sight left her feeling both excited and hopeful.

Within seconds, Clark returned with a bottle of pinot noir in one hand and a large melamine bowl filled with Italian chopped salad in the other.

"Can I help with anything?" she asked, scooting away from the table.

"Absolutely not. I've got this. You just relax."

Eva observed his confident prowl as he left the room, his gym-honed body looking magnificent from the back. This time, he came back carrying a basket filled with garlic bread and a large dish containing something unknown.

"Mmm, that smells good. What is it?"

"Smoked salmon over linguini with tomato cream sauce."

"It looks delicious."

"I hope it will be."

After pouring the wine and preparing their plates, Clark took a seat and raised his glass. "A toast. To the great work you're doing at Fremont General, us continuing to enjoy each other's company, and exploring whatever the future may hold."

"Cheers."

He ran his fingertips across the top of her hand, sending sensations straight up her thighs. Slowly lowering her glass, Eva squirmed in her chair, wondering how she was going to get through dinner.

"So, what do you think?" Clark asked before biting into a piece of garlic bread.

"It's amazing. The salmon is practically melting inside my mouth."

His right eyebrow shot up. "Hmm. Glad to hear it. I'm looking forward to *you* melting inside my mouth later."

A forkful of pasta slithered down Eva's throat. She downed a gulp of wine, praying she wouldn't choke to death. If Clark didn't stop with the sexy innuendos, she'd probably expire on the spot.

"Question," she began in an attempt to steer the conversation in a more wholesome direction. "What do you think is going on between Leo and Brandi? It seems to me that they're into each other."

"Well, I can't speak for Brandi, but I definitely think Leo is into her. And while he can be a bit goofy at times, Leo's a good guy. So, who knows. Maybe he has a chance."

"They'd definitely make an interesting couple. With her sass and his quirk? The fun times and joke-telling would be never-ending."

"Sort of like us back in the day."

Eva looked up from the spool of linguini entwining her fork. His statement came off as lighthearted, joyful even. But the intensity behind Clark's penetrating stare told a different story—one that highlighted both the good and bad plotlines woven throughout their relationship.

"Speaking of our past…" he continued.

Uh-oh. Here we go again…

"Working alongside you has brought back so many memories of our time together during our residency. Do you have a favorite moment that we experienced during one of our rotations?"

"Oh, I love that question." Eva's eyes narrowed as her head tilted toward the ceiling. "It had to have been that time you and I were assigned to the ER, and a woman came in with her husband, thinking she had a stomach tumor. Remember that?"

"I do. She came in doubled over from severe back pain, had gained a lot of weight really quickly, and had been urinating frequently."

"Exactly. Poor thing. She was convinced she had ovarian cancer then found out she was three months pregnant."

"*After* being told she couldn't conceive." A glow of happiness surrounding Clark's smile. "Yeah, that moment was beautiful. I remember her husband crying because they'd just begun the adoption process. He was so happy that they'd be welcoming two children into the family instead of one."

"Stories like that make our work well worth it. What about you? What's one of your favorite moments from our med school days?"

"Well, other than the obvious," he quipped with a wink, "I'd say it was the time we were in the emergency room, and an older woman was rushed in who'd suffered a stroke. She was babysitting at the time, and it was her three-year-old grandson who'd called 911 after she'd stopped responding to him during a game of go fish."

"Yes! I remember that patient. Had it not been for that bright, quick-thinking little boy, she wouldn't have survived."

They were suddenly interrupted by the ping of Clark's phone. The moment he grabbed it, Eva felt a pinch of envy pull at her chest.

No strings attached, remember? Whoever's messaging him is none of your business...

"Ha!" He chuckled after glancing at the screen.

"What's so funny?"

"That's Leo texting me. He said that while I'm out here living my best life with you, he's busy losing all his money to some of his poker buddies."

"*Ouch.* So, wait, you told Leo about us?"

"Not in detail. But Leo's a sharp guy. He could sense that something is going on."

"And that's *your* fault. You were being way

too obvious at the hospital. But now that the cat is somewhat out the bag, tell me. What does Leo think of us?"

Clark set his fork down and rubbed his hands together. "Put it this way. He has an interesting take on you and me."

"What do you mean?"

"Well, he knows some things about our past, and what brought you here to Las Vegas. I think he's hoping that more will come of us than what we've got planned. I don't think Leo understands our need to keep things casual."

You mean your need to keep things casual?

The words lingered on the tip of Eva's tongue. But she swallowed them down right along with a mouthful of lettuce. "Did you remind him that I'm only here for three months? And that you've got a certain...*lifestyle* that seems to suit you better than settling down with one woman—"

Clark broke into a fit of coughs.

"Are you all right?"

He responded with a heave so deep that Eva sprang from her chair and pounded his back. Once the coughing fit subsided, she ran into the kitchen and grabbed a bottle of water. As he gulped it down, she massaged his chest and back simultaneously.

"Thanks," he wheezed. "I don't know what just happened."

"I thought I was gonna have to take *you* to the ER."

"Please. If something goes wrong and a doctor of your caliber is in the house, I wouldn't need to step foot inside a hospital."

"Aww, you're just saying that because this massage feels so good."

"That it does," Clark responded, sliding his hand underneath her dress.

She leaned into him, closing her eyes as his fingers climbed higher. They touched the edge of her black lace thong, then slipped past the seam and skimmed her core.

Gasping slightly, Eva tightened her grip on his back.

"Why are you so wet?" he whispered.

"Because I've been sitting across from you for almost an hour."

"Mmm," he moaned, removing his hand and slowly licking his fingers. "Are you ready for dessert?"

"Most definitely. What are we having?"

"Tiramisu."

Eva tossed her head back and laughed. "Are you going off script? Because that's not where I thought this conversation was going."

"Oh, it isn't?" He stood, his wrinkled expression feigning confusion. "What did you think I was gonna say?"

"Use your imagination," she retorted, helping him carry the dishes into the kitchen.

As he stood over the dishwasher, she noticed the bulge inside his pants.

"I've got an idea," she said.

"Let's hear it."

"Why don't we hold off on dessert so you can give me a tour of your condo? Starting with the bedroom?"

Clark shot straight up and slammed the dishwasher door shut. "Good idea. That tiramisu isn't going anywhere."

Eva fell back against Clark's black leather sleigh bed. He tore at her dress as she ripped off his shirt. Her mouth roamed his chest, bit at his neck, savored remnants of fruity wine on his lips. Their tongues danced while their hands caressed every inch of each other. She reached between his legs, desperate to feel him inside her.

Clark pushed her hand away, a wicked chuckle tickling her ear. "Not yet," he grunted. Holding her wrists behind her back, he ran his tongue along the edge of her lobes, down her throat and along her collarbone. She arched her back, beating her fists against the sheets as grazed her skin with his teeth. Nipped at her inner thighs. Then devoured her toes, one by one, then all at once.

Eva grabbed Clark by the shoulders, urging him to come back up and satisfy her fully. But he refused, enjoying the tease. Relishing the control he had over her—the power to decide how close she'd come to climaxing. *When* she would climax. How hard her body would quiver once he finally allowed it.

She writhed about as Clark climbed halfway up the bed, his face getting lost between her thighs. The slightest touch of his tongue sent her shivering, but not fully. The tip of his finger tickling her opening ever so slightly, causing a scream to erupt from her throat.

Eva clawed at his back, attempting to inflict just enough pain so that he'd have mercy on her. He didn't. Instead, he crawled up toward the headboard and straddled her face, his knees on either side of her head.

"Open wide."

The pleasure that his command induced almost caused her to weep. Where was this confident, take-charge man back in the day? And why had it taken Eva so long to discover how much she enjoyed being dominated in bed?

Because you'd been with a man who barely enjoyed sex...

Clark reached down and placed a hand on her jaw. "Did you hear what I said? Open wide!"

Eva did as she was told. Clark emitted a guttural moan, still carefully holding her face while she tightened her jaws around him. Determined to maintain some semblance of control, she suppressed a gag as he slid down the back of her throat.

He began to pulsate inside her mouth. His thrusts grew stronger, faster. Just when she thought he was about to explode, he pulled out and finally plunged deep inside her.

Their bodies thrust to the exact same rhythm, never once falling out of sync.

When Clark finally allowed her to come, every nerve in her body shook with ecstasy.

Eva rolled over onto his chest, struggling to catch her breath. Tonight had been exactly what she'd needed. There was no negative talk of their past. Or the challenges they'd faced inside the ER. Or life after her temp assignment ended. The evening had simply been about joy. Keeping things light. Relishing each other's company. And pleasing each other with no strings attached.

But the problem was that Eva still had such strong emotions about their situation. So strong that she knew she should've taken longer to consider the conditions of Clark's ground rules before agreeing to his terms.

CHAPTER ELEVEN

Month two

THE YVONNE'S HOUSE charity gala was in full swing. The organization's planning committee had created a magical atmosphere inside Château Le Jardin's elegant gold and cream La Parisienne ballroom. Soft lights illuminating from crystal chandeliers glowed against elevated floral arrangements. Red carpet lined the entryway, where a professional photographer snapped photos of guests as they entered the event. Beautifully dressed guests wearing an array of evening gowns and custom-fitted tuxedos filled every table.

As far as Clark was concerned, Eva was the most stunning woman there. When she'd stepped into her building's lobby, he'd almost fainted at the sight of her dressed in a strapless floor-length emerald gown. Its slit ended someone near her upper right thigh. The sweetheart neckline revealed the perfect hint of cleavage. Her hair, which had been pulled back into an elegant chignon, put her shimmery makeup, pavé drop earrings and slender neck on full display.

Clark could barely keep his hands off her. As the gala's jazz band performed their rendition of Bill Withers's "Just the Two of Us," he held Eva close while they swayed to the music.

"Did I mention how handsome you look tonight?" she asked.

"I can't remember. Because I've been too busy telling you how gorgeous you look. I owe Brandi big-time for convincing you to buy this dress."

"I thought it was a bit much with the high slit and low cleavage. However, if you like it, I love it."

"It's perfect. *You're* perfect."

"You are too sweet," she murmured. "Thank you."

Running his fingertip along her chin, he asked, "So what did Amanda say when you told her about us? I can only imagine how shocked she was to hear we're back on."

"You know, I've been so busy that I haven't had a chance to tell her yet."

"Really? I'm surprised. I expected you to call her the minute I left your place that first morning."

"By the time you actually walked out the door, I only had thirty minutes left to get to work, remember?"

"Well," Clark said slowly, "I'm sure your parents must've been surprised to hear we've reconnected. They were so skeptical of me back in the day, thinking I'd distract you from your studies and ruin your chances of becoming a hugely successful doctor. What did they have to say about us *both* being successful doctors now?"

Rolling her eyes, she uttered, "When it comes to my parents, I've kept the details of this entire Las Vegas situation under wraps. They didn't want me to accept the assignment in the first place. Honestly, I think they were hoping I'd stay in Black Willow and try to work things out with Kyle."

Clark's body stiffened. The response stung, leaving him feeling as though they were back in medical school and he still wasn't good enough for her. It served as a timely reminder that he didn't have Kyle's high-society Black Willow background that would elevate Eva even further in her parents' eyes. Their desire to see her marry into hometown royalty left him feeling even more determined to protect his heart and keep their fling temporary.

"Hey!" Leo called out while bouncing toward them. "You two enjoying yourselves?"

"We are," Eva said. "This venue is gorgeous, the filet mignon was delicious, and the band is fantastic. They're loads better than the one I'd hired to play at my wedding!"

Clark's grasp on Eva's back loosened at yet another reference to her ex-fiancé.

"So how are things going between you, Rita and Brandi?" she asked Leo.

"Great. Even better than I expected. After Rita saw me walk in here with someone else, she hasn't taken her eyes off me. She's barely even paying attention to that guy she's with. Wilbur, or whatever his name is."

"William," Clark interjected.

"Whatever. The point is my plan worked. So, thanks again for coming, and a *huge* thank-you for convincing Brandi to be my fake date."

"Of course," Eva said. "We'll always have your back. What are you thinking now? Is there a chance that you and Rita might get back together?"

"*Hell*, no! That's not what this is about."

"It isn't?"

Leo shook his head so vigorously that his jowls shook. "Absolutely not. This is about knowing that I could get her back if I wanted to."

"You're ridiculous, man," Clark said before turning to Eva. "I'm gonna head to the bar and grab another drink. Can I get you anything?"

"No, I'm fine. Thanks. I see Brandi standing on the red carpet and she's waving me over. She must want to snap some pictures. Can I catch back up with you a little later?"

"Of course."

Clark stood rigidly as she planted a quick kiss on his cheek, then rushed off.

"You good, man?" Leo asked, his head swiveling from Clark to Eva, then back to Clark.

"I'm fine," he muttered, ignoring the unease twisting through his gut while walking to the bar. After ordering two Manhattans, he and Leo settled in at a high-top table.

"I have something to admit," Leo said.

"What's that?"

"I think I'm into Brandi. I mean, *really* into her."

"Yeah, I already knew that."

"Huh? How could you? *I* didn't know that until tonight!"

"Oh, please. All that laughing and joking you two do at the hospital? It reeks of a *strong* attraction. And don't get me started on our nights out at the Oasis. But here's my question. What are you gonna do about it?"

"That I don't know," Leo declared while staring across the room at her. "I should be asking you for some advice. Because you and Eva wasted no time in getting together, in spite of your complicated past. What's your secret?"

"You don't wanna take any advice from me. Trust me, I don't have this whole dating thing figured out, either."

"What do you mean? You two seem to be doing great."

Clark responded with a tight side-eye before taking a long sip of his drink.

"Uh-oh. What the hell? You mean to tell me there's trouble in paradise already?"

"Let's just say that Eva's parents are really rooting for her to get back together with her ex-fiancé. And I'm concerned that their influence might override whatever this is we've got going on."

Leo rebutted, "Why do you care? Per *your* ground rules, you two are just keeping things casual, right? Then once Eva's temp assignment is over, you'll go your way and she'll go hers."

Clark's gaze drifted toward her, his groin stirring as she struck a seductive pose alongside Brandi. "Yep, that was the plan."

"*Was?* Humph. Judging by the scowl on your face, the plan isn't working out too well for you. Could it be that you actually want more with the woman you're clearly still madly in love with?"

Clark remained silent.

"See, I *knew* you weren't gonna be able to contain your feelings. And the thing is, you shouldn't! Eva is a good woman, Clark. Just be honest and tell her where you stand. What have you got to lose?"

"What have I got to lose? How about my pride. My emotions. My heart. Basically, *everything*. I've already put myself out there and gotten badly burned by her once. I'm not doing it again."

"Look, all that happened years ago. You two

kicked things off on a clean slate this time round, remember? Both of you deserve a second shot at this. Like I keep saying, you have got to open yourself up to love, man."

Clark downed his drink, then waved Leo off. "I've never been enough for Eva. I wasn't back when we first got together, and I'm not now."

"How do you know that?"

"Because she hasn't told the people she's closest to that we're involved. Her parents don't even know that we're working together. They still seem to be hung up on her ex, too."

Leo cocked his head to the side. "I'm sorry to break this to you, but that's usually how it goes when there are no strings attached, my friend. You wanted this to be a casual hookup, so that's exactly what Eva's giving you. Now that you want more, you need to tell her."

"*Tuh.* The only thing I need to do is get my head back in the game and stick to the ground rules that I laid down when Eva and I started this."

"Meaning going back to your casual dating ways?"

"Exactly."

CHAPTER TWELVE

"LET'S GET THE patient inside room 8," Clark shouted. "*Stat!* Where is Dr. Gordon?"

"Right here," she said, rushing toward the group of paramedics. "What's the situation with our patient?"

"She fell from a balcony located thirty feet above a large saltwater aquarium at the No Man's Land Amusement Park and landed inside the tank. She may be suffering from alcohol poisoning along with a slew of other injuries. According to the park's staff, the patient appeared intoxicated and was behaving erratically before falling in."

Brandi ran over and handed the doctors protective equipment. Urgency palpitated through the room as nurses and medical assistants poured inside.

"Make sure she's lying in the supine position with her head turned to the side!" Eva called out when paramedics transferred the patient onto the bed and disconnected her from the EMS monitors. "We don't want her choking on vomit, water or debris. Is she conscious?"

"Yes, but barely," one of the paramedics responded. "Her pulse is faint and her blood pressure is low."

Once Eva and Brandi cut the patient out of her wet clothing, they reattached the precordial leads to the chest stickers and clipped a pulse oximeter onto her fingertip.

While eyeing the monitor, Clark said, "Her blood pressure is ninety-four over sixty-two. We need to get that up immediately."

"Should we administer a dose of epinephrine?" Eva asked.

"That's exactly what I was thinking. Timothy?"

"I'm on it," the medical assistant replied before charging out of the room.

"Do we know how long the patient was underwater?" Clark asked.

"Anywhere between ten to fifteen minutes before the park staff pulled her out," Rian replied. "She was conscious before the fall but unresponsive once she was removed from the water. A park staff member performed CPR until the paramedics arrived."

Waves of adrenaline coursed through Eva's veins. She'd never treated an intoxicated, barely conscious near-drowning victim who was suffering from numerous injuries.

Stay calm. Clark is right by your side. You've got this.

Noticing the patient's cold, blue-tinged skin, Eva turned to Brandi and Rian. "We need to cover her in forced air-warming blankets to prevent hypothermia and administer warming IV fluids to avoid further heat loss and dehydration from the potential alcohol poisoning."

"Yes, Dr. Gordon."

Clark approached with an ophthalmoscope in hand. After switching on the instrument's light, he adjusted the diopter dial and peered into the patient's eyes through the viewing window.

"The patient's pupils are equal, but sluggish. There's movement in her limbs, which is good. We'll know more about her condition once we're able to perform neurological and neurophysiological examinations."

"I suggest we implement spinal precautions as well," Eva said, "just in case there's a cord injury that has yet to be detected. Do we know our patient's name?"

"Yes, Melissa Sullivan."

"Ms. Sullivan?" Eva said, leaning toward the bed. "I'm Dr. Gordon. You're in good hands here at Fremont General Hospital. The medical team and I are going to do everything we can to get you well, okay?"

She nodded, wheezing feebly. When a slight cough progressed into a gag, Eva quickly unstrapped the oxygen mask and turned the patient's head far to the left.

"I need an emesis basin!"

Rian grabbed the kidney-shaped container and positioned it underneath the patient's chin just as a combination of aspirated water, red algae and crushed coral poured from her mouth.

"Nurse Bennett," Clark said, "let's switch out that oxygen mask for a high-flow nasal cannula so that the patient's mouth will remain uncovered."

"Yes, Doctor."

Unwrapping the stethoscope from around her neck, Eva pressed the diaphragm against the patient's chest and listened to her lungs. The loud, low-pitched crackling indicated that fluid was present in the lungs.

"I'm detecting acute pulmonary edema. We need to perform chest X-rays and confirm that as soon as possible."

"We've got the mobile CT scanner here," Clark responded. "We'll get some images once the patient is stable. What is her blood pressure reading now?"

"It's dropped to ninety-one over sixty. We need that epinephrine. *Stat*."

"I've got it right here!" Timothy panted, rushing over and handing the pen to Clark.

He pulled the safety release from the auto-injector and held it firmly against the patient's outer right thigh.

"Wait," Eva said. "You're not administering the normal dose of one milligram, are you?"

"Absolutely not. Since the patient still has a pulse, that high a dosage could cause malignant hypertension and lead to cardiac arrest. So I'm administering a half of a milligram instead."

"Good. Just making sure."

The pair shared a brief glance, Eva beaming behind her mask when Clark tossed her an appreciative wink. She watched as he inserted the needle into the patient's leg, waited for it to click, then gave her a thumbs-up to confirm that the injection had begun.

"I'm holding the auto-injector in place for five seconds," Clark said, "to ensure that the epinephrine fully activates. Nurse Bennett, how is Ms. Sullivan's oxygen level looking?"

"Still low at sixty-seven percent."

"Is the humidified delivery set at one hundred percent with a flow rate of sixty liters per minute?"

"Yes, it is."

"Okay. Let's keep it there. A combination of the epinephrine and accelerated output should increase her oxygen level."

"And hopefully avoid a prolonged state of hypoxemia," Eva added. "We need to take every precaution that'll help prevent cardiac arrest."

Clark nodded, then pointed toward the mobile computed tomography scanner. "Rian, can you bring over the scanner? We need to perform that trauma CT and check for any initial neurologic or pulmonary injuries."

"You got it."

Despite the dire condition of the patient, Eva was overcome by a sense of ease. It was a level of comfort that she hadn't experienced since her and Clark's days of working together during medical school. Although she'd arrived at Fremont General second-guessing her decision to take on the assignment, his support and guidance had enabled Eva to find her footing and adapt quickly. His presence alone made her feel as though she could conquer anything. And while the city's patient cases had been both complicated and challenging, thanks to Clark, she'd risen to every occasion.

"Preparing to infuse the patient with iodine," he said, "then begin the scan—"

Beep! Beep! Beep!

Eva's eyes shot up toward the monitor. The patient's blood pressure had dropped to eighty-three over forty-one. When she began convulsing uncontrollably while gasping for air, Eva tore off the warming blankets.

"The patient has gone into cardiac arrest! Get the defibrillator. *Stat!*"

Eva exposed her bare chest and immediately

began performing CPR while Brandi positioned the defibrillator next to the bed. Grabbing the pads, Clark quickly removed the paper backing and pressed one below the patient's right-side clavicle and the other underneath her left armpit.

"Good job on the CPR, Dr. Gordon," he said while tapping the machine's energy selection button. "Keep that up while the defibrillator analyzes the patient's heart rhythm."

Clark set the biphasic energy level to two hundred joules and hit the charge button. It blinked red, indicating it was fully charged.

"Stand clear, everybody!"

Once the team had stepped away from the bed, he pressed the machine's *shock* button. The first shock was delivered. As the patient's shoulders shook slightly, Eva went right back in and began performing CPR.

"Come on…come on…" she whispered, sweat trickling down her forehead.

Two minutes passed. Eva paused while the team observed the monitor, assessing the patient's heart rhythm. The line tracing was primarily flat with waves that occasionally spiked and dipped. When the new pulse reading flashed on the screen, it came in at thirty-two.

"That heart rate is still too low," Clark stated. "Preparing to deliver another shock. Stand clear, everyone!"

A second dose of electric current shock was

administered. Eva proceeded with another round of CPR.

"Please, *please*," she begged, willing the patient to respond.

After another two minutes, Eva stopped the compressions once again. The team held their breath, hoping for a positive response.

"Ough!"

The patient emitted a hearty cough just as her eyes flew open.

"Yes!" Eva panted.

The machine beeped, a new set of vitals flashing on the screen.

"The patient's blood pressure and pulse rate are stabilizing," Clark announced. "Let's keep the defibrillator pads in place just in case those numbers drop again. Is the oxygenation still running at full speed?"

"Yes, Doctor," Brandi said.

Eva pulled the blankets farther down the bed. "The patient's temperature is ninety-seven degrees. We need to bring it down to somewhere between eighty-nine and ninety-three to prevent possible brain damage."

"Rian," Clark said, "grab some cooling pads. Those will help lower her temperature quickly." He turned to Eva. "Great work, Dr. Gordon."

"Same to you, Dr. Malone," she said, resisting the urge to embrace him as tears of relief burned her eyes. "Once the patient is transferred to the ICU, I'm thinking she should be placed in a medically induced coma to allow time for her body to recover."

"I agree. I'd also like to get those CT scans done as soon as possible so we'll know the extent of her injuries."

"Doctors?" Brandi called out. "The patient's vitals are continuing to normalize. Should I begin preparing for a transfer to the ICU?"

Clark blew an exhausted exhale, nodding his head. "Yes, please. Thank you, Nurse Bennett." He turned to Eva. "Today was a tough one. I'm glad you were here, working alongside me."

"So am I. But I'm sure you would have done just fine without me."

He gave her hand a squeeze. "Maybe. Thank goodness I didn't have to find out."

Once the patient had been transported to the ICU, Eva joined Clark at the surgical sink.

"I am exhausted," she sighed before leaning over and whispering, "I cannot wait to slip out of these scrubs and in between the sheets with you. Dinner and drinks at my place tonight?"

"Mmm, that sounds nice…"

"I was thinking about whipping up a teriyaki-glazed chicken stir-fry, some spicy garlic edamame, sautéed French green beans—"

"But I can't," Clark interrupted.

Eva's hands froze underneath the stream of water. "I'm sorry. You what?"

"I can't get together with you tonight. I have plans."

"Uh…" Eva uttered. "Okay."

She waited for him to elaborate. He didn't. Instead, Clark backed away from the sink.

"Thanks again for today," he told her. "You were amazing in there. See you in the morning?"

She forced a nod. "Yep. See you tomorrow."

Clark turned his attention toward the rest of the team. "Great job today, everyone. I appreciate all the hard work and quick thinking." And with that, he exited the emergency room.

Eva just stood there, watching him leave.

"You okay?" Brandi asked, her gaze drifting from Clark's back to Eva's baffled expression.

"I'm fine. It's just…it's been a long day. I was looking forward to hanging out with Clark tonight, but apparently he has other plans."

"Well, Leo and I are going to the Oasis to grab drinks tonight. Why don't you join us?"

"Thanks, but I'll pass. I don't wanna disrupt your evening. You two go on and have a good time. I'll be fine."

"Are you sure?"

"I'm positive," Eva lied.

After the cavalier brush-off from Clark, she was far from fine.

CHAPTER THIRTEEN

"HAVE YOU HEARD the news? Your ex-fiancé won the election," Amanda said, her tone as dry as the Mojave Desert.

"Yeah, I know."

Eva's cell pinged loudly in her ear once again. Ever since Kyle had been declared the winner of Iowa's senatorial race last night, her phone had been blowing up.

"Everyone knows that Kyle and I aren't together anymore. I don't know why they feel the need to reach out with congratulatory calls and messages."

"Maybe that's their way of trying to bring you two back together."

"Starting with my very own mother. *And* his. Not only have they both called to inform me of the win, but according to my cousin, they're ready to resume the wedding planning."

"Okay, now they're going way too far."

Eva plopped down on the couch and slipped on her sneakers. It was her day off, and she'd decided to make it all about her. A nice run in the park, a little shopping, a few rounds of blackjack at Aria followed by a Cantonese lobster dinner at Catch. Since she'd been in Vegas, most of her days had been spent inside Fremont General's emergency room, while the nights had been dedicated to Clark. But Clark had been pulling away from her recently, and Eva figured she should dedicate more of it to herself.

"Look, enough about Kyle," Amanda said. "How are things going between you and Clark?"

"Um…they're cool. I guess…"

"Just cool, you guess? Well, that doesn't sound very convincing."

"Listen, there's something I need to tell you. And just know that I didn't mention it sooner because I didn't want you to make a bigger deal out of it than what it is."

"Okay, I'm listening."

Eva leaned against the back of the couch and squeezed her eyes shut. "Clark and I have been sleeping together."

"I knew it!" Amanda screamed so loudly that Eva almost dropped the phone. "The way you kept disappearing at night and not taking my calls, then acting all coy when I asked about him. Why would you withhold something like that from me?"

"Because I didn't want you to get your hopes up! It's nothing. Just a friends-with-benefits type of situation that's going to end once my temp assignment is over."

"But if I know you like I think I do," Amanda said, "I'm assuming the feelings you've always had for Clark have intensified, haven't they?"

"Yes." Eva stood and began pacing the floor. "Not to mention the sex is *amazing.* Ever since Clark and I opened up to each other about everything that went down in the past and started over fresh, I've wanted to see where things would go between us. Explore something deeper. But he seems to be against any sort of commitment. Clark is the one who insisted we keep things casual in the first place. Instead of us getting closer as time goes on, he's actually been keeping me more at an emotional distance. And I don't know why, but whenever I try to talk about anything meaningful, he brushes me off."

"And you haven't pressed the issue about wanting more?"

Eva schlepped over to the mirror and pulled her hair into a high ponytail, then swiped on a coat of clear lip gloss. "I haven't. I guess I just assumed it would happen naturally. You know how close Clark and I were back in the day. Maybe that had me convinced he'd eventually change his mind and want something more, too. Clearly I was wrong. And that's fine. I won't be in Las Vegas forever. I'll just focus on finishing out my assignment then get back home to the real world."

Huffing into the phone, Amanda replied, "Easier said than done, my friend. I think you and Clark feel the exact same way about each other, but neither of you are willing to admit it. And you know how men are. Once they've been hurt, it's hard for them to bounce back. He's afraid. Convince him that you won't run away this time. The man loves you. Don't let this second chance pass you by. If you do, I promise you'll regret it."

Eva grabbed her keys and headed for the door, ignoring the pangs of frustration rattling her rib cage. "One thing you're right about is that I hurt Clark before, and I don't think he'll ever let that go. Maybe keeping his guard up while dating around is his way of getting back at me. Whatever the case may be, I'm not about to try to force a man to want me. I refused to do it with Kyle, and I won't do it with Clark. And on that note, I love you, but I need to get this run in to clear my head."

"I love you, too. And I hear what you're saying. But please, just take what I'm saying into consideration before you completely write Clark off."

"I'll think about it. Bye."

Eva disconnected the call and headed down to the lobby. When the elevator doors opened, she saw someone standing at the concierge's desk behind a huge bouquet of pink peonies.

"Aww, how sweet," she whispered, her tongue stinging with envy.

"I'm not sure of the apartment number," a familiar voice said, "but the name is Eva Gordon. *Dr.* Eva Gordon."

She stopped so abruptly that the soles of her sneakers almost sent her crashing to the floor.

"What's *my* name?" the man asked the concierge. "Senator Kyle Benson."

Eva's stomach dropped to her knees. She quickly pivoted, rushing back toward the elevators. On the way there, she skidded across the freshly polished floors, grabbing hold of the couch's armrest before almost hitting the marble tiles.

Footsteps charged in her direction. "Dr. Gordon?" the concierge asked. "Are you all right?"

Kyle was right behind him. "Hey, there's my girl!"

She stood, straightening her bright pink tank top. "I'm fine, Mr. Jackson. Thank you. Kyle, what in the world are you doing here?"

"What do you mean? I'm here to celebrate my senatorial win with my future wife!"

Mr. Jackson's expression wrinkled with bewilderment. "I will, um... I'll give you two some privacy," he uttered before returning to the front desk. He'd gotten to know Clark quite well during his frequent visits to the building. Eva could only imagine what the concierge was thinking.

In that moment, however, his opinion was the least of her concerns.

Kyle approached with open arms. She studied his face, noticing that the stress of the election had completely dissipated. Gone were the dark circles surrounding his eyes and hunched shoulders plagued with the weight of the campaign. He appeared brighter. Lighter on his feet as he flashed her a genuine, carefree smile.

Pressing his lips somewhere between Eva's cheek and mouth, then stepping away, Kyle oozed confidence as he straightened his perfectly tailored gray blazer.

"But before you start interrogating me," Kyle said, "here's a question for you. What in the world are *you* doing here? In Las Vegas of all places. Oh, and on a side note, I shouldn't have had to find out from your mother that you'd moved across the country."

"First of all, I didn't move here. I accepted a three-month assignment at Fremont General Hospital. Secondly, why would I go out of my way to inform you of anything? You broke off our engagement to focus on your campaign, remember? I figured you'd be too busy to care where I went."

"Come on, E. That was just a break, not a *breakup*. You knew we'd get back together once I won the election."

"I didn't know that, actually."

"The time apart was obviously worth it, because you're standing before the new senator of Iowa! And where am I right now, when I should be back home celebrating with my people? I'm here, with you. Because *you're* the only one who I really wanted to share this moment with."

The air thickened around Eva as Kyle led her toward the front desk. When he reached for the floral arrangement, she spun a full turn, suddenly anxious to escape the lobby.

"Eva, what's wrong? Are you okay?"

"I just… I need some air."

She hurried through revolving doors and headed straight to the neighboring coffee shop.

"Sir!" Kyle called out to the concierge. "Can you please keep an eye on those flowers for me?"

His hard-soled oxford shoes clicked along the pavement as he ran after Eva.

"Baby," he panted, grabbing hold of her. "Talk to me. I know this must be a lot, me popping up unannounced."

"Ya think?" she shot back. "I'm overwhelmed, to say the least. We haven't spoken since that night at Chateau Eilean. So, yes. I'm gonna need a minute."

Raising his hands in surrender, Kyle backed off. "I understand."

Eva allowed him to open the café's frosted glass door. She stepped inside, cool air settling into her damp skin as the rich aroma of roasted coffee beans floated through the air. The rustic shop usually served as a place of calm after a long day at the hospital. But today, there was nothing the low lighting, neutral color palette and lush plants could do to soothe her chaotic mind.

She approached the counter and ordered an iced black coffee. Kyle told the barista to make it two and rushed to pay for their drinks.

"Look," he said, following her to the end of the bar. "Just hear me out. I am beyond sorry for the way I handled things back in Black Willow. You have no idea how many nights I've spent wishing I could turn back time and change what I did. I shouldn't have allowed my campaign to take over and in the process, given up on us. I will forever regret it. Winning that election doesn't mean as much to me as I thought it would, because I don't have you by my side."

Eva stared at him blankly, as if she couldn't quite comprehend his words. Never had Kyle spoken to her with that much heart. And in the five years they were together, she couldn't even remember a time when he'd apologized for anything.

"Despite the fact that I'm still angry with you," she said, "I can appreciate you saying that. So… thank you."

After the barista handed them their drinks, Kyle pointed to the outdoor patio. "It's a beautiful day. Why don't we sit outside and talk?"

They settled in at a table facing her building. Kyle stared into the lobby and waved, giving the concierge a thumbs-up. "Just making sure he doesn't let anybody touch your flower arrangement. Does it look familiar?"

"It does, ironically. That display is very similar to one of the options I'd chosen for our wedding."

Kyle leaned back, his lips spreading into a toothy smile. "Yeah, I know."

"What do you mean, you *know*? You couldn't have remembered a thing about our wedding plans considering you weren't interested in them."

"Welp, obviously I was. Because I remember you showing me something that looked just like the arrangement sitting on your concierge's desk."

Confusion pounded inside Eva's head. Who was this smooth-talking man with the self-assured gleam? Kyle the politician always knew how to turn it on for the people. The charm. The warmth. The wit. Until now, Eva hadn't realized just how distant he'd become toward her behind closed doors. In this moment, however, he lit up the entire patio, exuding love and redemption.

Don't fall for it...

Sliding his chair closer to hers, Kyle said, "I can only imagine how eager you are to return to Black Willow."

"Hmm, I don't know. I'm really enjoying my

188 ER DOC'S LAS VEGAS REUNION

time here in Las Vegas. The weather is great,
there's always something to do, and working at
Fremont General has been really rewarding. I've
learned so much while treating patients with conditions I never thought I'd face."

Talk of the hospital brought on thoughts of
Clark. Where was he? Who was he with? What
were they doing? An image of him lying in bed
with another woman flashed through her head.
Eva squeezed her eyes shut, hoping the pressure
would dissolve the visual.

"I can understand that," Kyle continued. "I
love a good challenge, too. But this place isn't
you, Eva. This town reeks of alcohol and mari-
juana. Ringing slot machines and cheap sex. A
distinguished, intelligent, classy woman like you
doesn't belong here."

"Let me stop you right there. You can't speak
on this city as if it's just some seedy underworld.
Las Vegas has plenty to offer other than drinking, gambling and partying. It is a hub for eco-
nomic development. The job market is booming,
the technological endeavors are flourishing, the
educational, social service and health care sys-
tems are advancing—"

Gently placing his hand over hers, Kyle in-
terjected, "Listen to me, honey. That's not what
I'm saying. The point is, this place isn't Black
Willow. You're a huge part of our hometown and

a pillar of the community. Your patients miss you. Your family misses you. More importantly, *I* miss you. Things will be good between us again now that the pressure is off me."

Eva slid her hand out from underneath Kyle's grasp. "You can't just assume that. Now you've won the election, it's time for the real work to begin. Who's to say you won't leave me again when things get tough? Because they will, you know."

Kyle turned away, blowing an exasperated sigh.

"What's gonna happen when a bill you're pushing doesn't get passed? Or a federal judge you're supporting doesn't get appointed? With all the Senate sessions, meetings with constituents, committee hearings and the list goes on, your workload is going to be extremely hectic."

"I know, I know. Leave all that up to me, Eva. I can handle it. And I can handle us. Now, when is this little temp thing you're doing going to be over so you can come back home, take over as my first lady, and put the wedding plans back in motion?"

She fell back against her chair in shock. "Do you really think us getting back together is going to be that easy?"

"Why wouldn't it be?"

Eva rolled her eyes, her head swiveling in the

opposite direction. A familiar-looking car appeared in the near distance. It was a midnight-blue Mercedes, pulling out of her building's driveway.

"Wait, is that...?" she whispered. After a brief moment, she muttered, "Oh, hell!" and crouched down underneath the table.

Kyle stood and reached inside his pocket. "Listen, sweetheart. How about I show you just how easy this can be rather than tell you?"

He got down on one knee as Eva stooped in front of him, peering over his shoulder.

"Eva," he continued before pulling out a small black velvet box.

"Wh—what is that?" she asked her eyes wide. "What are you doing?"

He opened it, revealing a huge princess-cut solitaire so brilliant that it set off light beams underneath the bright Las Vegas sun.

"It's a new engagement ring," Kyle said. "To represent our new start. Come on, babe," he crooned, taking her hand in his. "It's me and you against the world. Or Iowa at least. Dr. Eva Gordon, will you accept my proposal once again and marry me?"

The piercing squeal of tire treads screeched in front of the coffee shop. Eva turned toward the curb. There, staring her dead in the face through the windshield, was Clark.

Her knees shook as she attempted to stand. She looked on in horror as Clark tore off his sunglasses with a sneer so contemptuous that it sent chills straight through her.

Kyle was too busy slipping the ring on her finger to notice a thing.

It's not what you think! she tried to call out.

But her vocal cords were numb with shock. Grabbing Kyle by the shoulders, she rasped, "Help me up!"

Instead, he pulled her closer. She fell into him, involuntarily wrapping her arms around his back as she struggled not to tumble to the ground.

"I knew you'd come around, baby," Kyle gushed, embracing her tightly. "I *knew* you'd come around!" He pulled her up, raising her left hand in the air and yelling, "We're getting married, people. We're getting married! *Whoo!*"

The small crowd sitting around them broke into applause.

"Will you please let me go!" Eva gritted out after finally finding her voice. She wiggled away from Kyle and jetted toward the curb. But it was too late. Clark had already pulled off.

Kyle approached with his phone in hand and began snapping photos of her. "I cannot wait to send these pics to our moms. They are gonna be ecstatic. I need to call the *Black Willow Herald*, too, and let them know that the wedding is back on. The news will be on the front page tomorrow. Turn around and face me, E. And smile!"

Eva staggered into the street, barely hearing a word Kyle was saying. She was too busy watching Clark speed off into the distance.

CHAPTER FOURTEEN

CLARK STARED AT his reflection in Posh Fit Gym's mirror, heaving as he lifted a fifty-pound dumbbell over his head. The anger pulsating through his veins had him seeing double. He squeezed his eyes shut, pushing past the burn of his sixth set of reps while hoping the pain would numb his feelings.

Leo, who was laid out on the floor next to Clark, had been stretching his calves for the past twenty minutes. Wiggling onto his side, he panted, "So let me get this straight. You and Eva agreed to see other people if you wanted to, but you have yet to go out with anyone else, even if she thinks you have?"

"Yes. Because I haven't come across anyone who I'm interested in dating."

"Or maybe it's because you can't get Eva out of your head. She's the only woman you want. The sooner you can admit that yourself, the better off you'll be."

"Like I said," Clark huffed, increasing the

speed on his bicep curls, "no one has caught my attention."

"Is that the story we're going with?"

"Yes. Because it's the truth. Look, while you're so busy grilling me, why don't you admit to whatever's going on between you and Brandi?"

Leo rolled back over and pulled his knees into his chest. "Brandi and I are cool. We're hanging out. Enjoying each other's company. You know what I mean?"

"So you two are dating."

"I didn't say all that. We're simply going with the flow. Now, have we shared a kiss or two? Yeah, we have."

"Okay then!" Clark said, tossing him a high five. "I like you two together—"

"Hold up, see, now you're going too far. Brandi and I are not officially together. And by the way, this conversation never happened. I promised her I'd keep things under wraps. Now, back to you. I'd like to know why you decided to stop by Eva's place without calling first."

"Dude, I told you that she and her ex got back together, and *that's* what you're focusing on?"

"All I'm saying is that when you roll up on someone unannounced, you've got to expect the unexpected. And maybe what you *think* you saw wasn't what you *actually* saw."

"Wait…*what*?" Clark shouted, cringing at the abrupt outburst. His eyes roamed the immediate area. No one was standing close enough to hear him lose his usual cool. "What I saw was him proposing, and the two of them hugging it out."

"That's impossible. Because last I heard, Eva couldn't stand the man. He's the main reason why she left Black Willow. Why would she take him back so easily?"

Clark dropped the dumbbells onto the floor, oblivious to the sonic boom that erupted from the crash. An urge to overexert himself took over. He jumped high in the air then hit the mat, releasing a series of burpees. "Because he's the new state senator of Iowa. And as we both know, Eva is a parent-pleaser. That's what they want. And I guess being with a stiff robot who's all about his image works for her, too."

"Well, you weren't presenting her with a better offer, so…" Leo flipped over on to his stomach and attempted to lift his head and chest up off the mat. "Check out my new yoga move. Upward facing dog. See, while you're over there killing yourself, I'm partaking in a much more effective workout that won't ruin my joints and—" He paused, dropped back down and pointed over at Clark. "Wait, how do you even know that Eva's ex won the election?"

Clark responded with a grunt as he broke into a set of jumping jacks.

"Aww, come on, man! Please tell me you

haven't gone back to your old ways. Are you using the internet to stalk Eva's life again?"

When Clark failed to reply once again, Leo rolled his eyes.

"Listen. As your best friend, I'm not gonna lie here and tell you what you wanna hear. I'm gonna tell you what you *need* to hear. This is all your fault."

"*My* fault?"

"Yes, *your* fault! You continue to let your past, not to mention old fears, get in the way of your future happiness. Your feelings for Eva haven't changed since med school. You may have suppressed them over the years, but they exploded the day she showed up at Fremont General. And how do you handle it? By coming at her with that dumb *no strings attached* rule. I don't think either of you really wanted that, but for whatever reason you both agreed to it. And look at you now. In denial and drowning your sorrows in sweat."

Exhausted both mentally and physically, Clark plopped down onto a nearby weight bench. He grabbed a towel and wiped his face, then bit into it in frustration. "Eva is an intelligent, outspoken woman. If she wanted more, she would've said that. I honestly think she sees this whole Las Vegas experience for exactly what it is—a temporary assignment. She's here to learn all she can and have a good time. Once the three months are up, she'll go back to her life in Black Willow and walk down the aisle with that clown."

"Here's a thought. Why don't you just ask her what's really going on?"

"Nope," Clark uttered defiantly, hitting the floor and cranking out a set of push-ups. "Absolutely not. When it comes down to it, Eva owes me nothing. We weren't in an exclusive relationship. If she wants me to know what's happening, she'll tell me."

That's what his mouth said. But when thoughts of Eva marrying another man rushed through his mind, Clark became sick to his stomach. The clean slate they'd established was getting muddier by the minute.

Grabbing his water bottle, Leo took a long drink and said, "Let me ask you this again. Why *did* you go over to Eva's?"

Clark acted as if he hadn't heard him, instead focusing on the floor as he pulled his right hand behind his back and pushed down with his left.

"Oh, feel free to stay silent while you show out with the one-handed push-ups. I already know the answer. You went there to tell her how you feel. Confess that you don't want to be with anyone but her. But then you saw Eva with her ex and backed off. So what now? Are you just gonna let her walk out of your life once again without putting up a fight?"

"That's exactly what I'm gonna do. You know

why? Because some things never change. Eva showed me who she was back in the day. A *runner*. She ran during med school because she was afraid to give us a chance. Ran from Black Willow when she couldn't face the heat after her relationship ended with a man she never really loved in the first place. And now she's gonna run back home when she's done here and pick right back up where she left off. How would I look trying to stop her when she's proven once again that I'm not the one for her?"

"But for the time being, Eva is still here. So stop ignoring your feelings. And drop that ridiculous *no strings attached* plan. The only reason you set it up in the first place was to avoid getting hurt. And in the end, you *still* got hurt."

Clark flinched underneath the sting of Leo's words. He racked his brain for a snappy response but came up empty. Because his friend was absolutely right.

Clark threw on his lab coat and rushed down the hallway. He was two minutes shy of being late for handoffs thanks to Leo, who'd insisted on ordering a second breakfast to go before leaving the restaurant.

After checking the schedule, Clark was relieved to see that he was on duty with Dr. Abrams instead of Eva. He knocked on the conference room door and headed inside. "Dr. Beal! I am so sorry I'm late—"

Clark stopped mid-sentence. There, sitting across from Dr. Beal, was Eva.

What in the hell are you doing here?

He swallowed the urge to blurt the first words that came to mind and cleared his throat, slowly closing the door behind him.

Pull it together. You are not that young, vulnerable med school student anymore. Fremont General is your house. Handle yourself accordingly.

"Dr. Gordon," he said, his tone laced with feigned indifference. "Good morning. I thought you were off today."

"Good morning, Dr. Malone. I was called in at the last minute. Dr. Abrams had to leave town unexpectedly, so I'm filling in for him."

Her cool tone was unnerving. Clark walked stiffly toward the chair next to Dr. Beal, his eyes darting in every direction except Eva's.

"No worries, Dr. Malone," Dr. Beal said. "I was just updating Dr. Gordon on a very complicated patient who checked into the ER last night. His name is Flex Cuttington, and he's a professional bodybuilder."

"Hence the name," Clark said wryly.

Eva, emitting that adorable giggle she knew drove him crazy, added, "I said the same thing. Check out this photo I found of him online."

She slid her cell phone across the table. Clark caught it, eyeing the shredded, deeply tanned man with bulging oiled-up muscles standing on-stage in a front double biceps pose.

"Wow..." Clark rasped. "He is huge. Does the man have time to do anything else besides work out? From the looks of him, he lives in the gym."

"Yeah, well, don't give him too much credit for time spent on the weight machines," Dr. Beal replied. "Mr. Cuttington owes plenty of this muscle mass to the black-market androgen and anabolic steroids he's been injecting into his delts, biceps, quads and glutes."

"Trenbolone, Superdrol and methyltrienolone to be exact," Eva interjected.

"Oh, no. Three of the most dangerous steroids out there, especially if they're administered incorrectly." Clark slid Eva's phone back to her. Before doing so, the thought of swiping through her text messages and call log crossed his mind, just to see how much she'd been communicating with Kyle. He thrust the distasteful thought away. He'd never do that.

When she caught her cell, their eyes met briefly. He waited for those dazzling hazel specks to shoot him a look of defiance. One that said she'd gotten the best of him yet again. That she had beaten him at his own game. A game for which he'd set the rules. But they didn't. Instead,

Eva's gaze was soft. Open. Wide with defense-lessness. Which left him confused.

Don't fall for it. Do not allow this beguiling woman's charms to take you down again.

Shifting his focus back to their patient, Clark asked, "So what brought Mr. Cuttington into the ER?"

"Well, he's preparing for a national bodybuilding competition," Dr. Beal responded. "In doing so, he's been stacking all three of the steroids that Dr. Gordon mentioned."

"Wait, you mean to tell me he's been shooting trenbolone, Superdrol and methyltrienolone at the same time?"

"Yes. And what's even more alarming is that he wasn't under any sort of dosage supervision. So he'd been using his own judgment when administering the injections. Now I will give Mr. Cuttington credit for doing some online research on the recommended dosages. However, since he wanted to bulk up quickly for that competition, he'd decided to triple the suggested amounts. After suffering two seizures and a racing heart-beat, his wife urged him to come to the hospital."

"He's lucky that didn't kill him," Clark said while reviewing the patient's chart. "I see here what the patient was hoping that method would do for him. The trenbolone was used to gain muscle and burn fat faster, Superdrol to retain lean muscle tissue and build stamina, and methyltrienolone to increase testosterone production and provide quick visible enhancements."

Eva slid a set of photos and CT scans toward Clark. "That was his plan. But as a result of his misuse, he's suffered a number of illnesses and injuries."

"And that's due to the dangerous combination of all three steroids, the high dosages he'd been administering, as well as the prolonged use of them," Dr. Beal chimed in.

Studying the photos of Mr. Cuttington, Clark noticed several open wounds on his shoulders, biceps, thighs and buttocks. Some were yellow and loose, with fluid oozing from the centers. Others were black, the tissue appearing thick and leathery.

"So the patient was injecting steroids directly into the muscles he was looking to build," Clark commented, "which caused skin necrosis."

"Exactly. We treated the wounds by first removing the dead tissue, then using hyperbaric oxygen therapy to speed up the healing process and improve organ function. I've been monitoring his blood pressure and heart rate as they're both running high, managing them with intravenous metoprolol."

"What dosage are you administering?"

Dr. Beal pushed his rimless bifocals up the bridge of his nose while thumbing through his notebook. "Let's see. I know I wrote that information down somewhere in here…"

"I recorded it earlier when we reviewed the patient's medical care plan," Eva said.

As she scrolled through the Notes app on her phone, Clark glanced down at her left hand. It was ringless.

She must've left it at home so as not to draw attention to herself.

Smart move. Clark wouldn't have been able to even look at her had she flaunted her rekindled engagement in his face.

"Here it is," she continued. "When the patient first arrived in the ER, Dr. Beal administered a five-milliliter bolus injection three times over the course of fifteen minutes. Once the patient's blood pressure stabilized, it was recommended that he begin taking one hundred milligram tablets twice daily."

"Thank you, Dr. Gordon," Dr. Beal said. "As for the seizures, I treated them with an intravenous infusion of levetiracetam."

"And what was the dosage on that?" Clark asked.

"Um…" Dr. Beal uttered, once again paging through his notebook.

"Ten milliliters," Eva said, "mixed with one hundred milliliters of sodium chloride. We're still waiting for the lab results from Mr. Cuttington's endocrine panel. My guess is that his extreme steroid use has wreaked havoc on his hormones. Oh, and after the infusion of levetiracetam, the patient was prescribed the same medication in pill form. One thousand milligrams, twice daily."

Dr. Beal gave Eva a nod of thanks before taking a long sip of coffee from his *Best Doctor Dad Ever* mug. "As you two can probably tell, it's been a long night. Plus, I'm coming off a twenty-four-hour shift. Once again, thank you for that, Dr. Gordon. You are beyond impressive, and it has really been a pleasure working with you."

She smiled, those pretty lips setting off a massive explosion below Clark's belt. Dr. Beal was right about her. Eva was extraordinary. Always present. And never rattled. Even in anger, Clark had no choice but to finally admit that he was as much in love with her now as he'd ever been. And with that came the realization that he never should've diminished their reconnection to a casual fling.

"I appreciate that, Dr. Beal," she responded humbly. "Thank you."

Shifting in his chair, Clark shuffled the papers in his hands. "I can imagine you're exhausted, Dr. Beal, so we won't hold you much longer. I'm looking over the patient's blood test, imaging and biopsy results, and they're showing kidney and liver damage. Have you established a treatment plan for those issues?"

"I have. Regarding the kidney damage, Mr. Cuttington has developed focal segmental glomerulosclerosis. I explained to him that this scarring within his kidneys is a direct result of the excessive steroid usage, and that it can be reversed if he discontinues use. I'm treating the damage with losartan to reduce the protein in his urine."

"Good," Clark added. "That'll help lower his blood pressure, too, along with the metoprolol."

"That's right. I'm also giving him atorvastatin to lower his cholesterol, which clocked in at two hundred and ninety-six, and furosemide to prevent water retention and swelling."

Leaning back in his chair, Dr. Beal closed his eyes and emitted a long sigh.

"You all right, Doc?" Clark asked.

"Yep. Just slowly drifting off into the abyss."

Eva gave Dr. Beal's arm a sympathetic pat, then passed a chart to Clark. "The patient is in stage two liver failure. The fibrosis is moderate since the scarred tissue hasn't replaced an excessive amount of healthy tissue. Dr. Beal explained to Mr. Cunningham that fibrosis is treatable as long as he discontinues use of the steroids. The furosemide he's taking for the kidney damage will also treat the liver as it'll remove excess fluid from the body. It's been recommended that the patient limit his salt intake, implement a healthy diet plan rich in vitamins D, E, C and B, and take a multivitamin daily."

"Got it," Clark said while rigorously jotting down notes. "Sounds like an excellent plan to me."

Dr. Beal burst into a round of applause. "Dr. Gordon, you are a rock star. I'm so glad you're here with Dr. Malone for this complicated hand-off." He nudged Clark's shoulder, then said to her, "Are you *sure* you can't stick around Fremont General after your temporary assignment is over? We sure could use someone of your caliber around here permanently."

"Thank you, Dr. Beal. But unfortunately, no. I haven't been asked to stay. Plus, I hear my family and the townspeople back in Black Willow miss me terribly."

Her words crumbled the wall of protection Clark had built around his heart. He'd tried hard to follow the rules they'd both agreed to. Keep his emotions at bay. Not catch feelings. And let their brief fling go once Eva's time in Las Vegas was up. But instead, he had completely failed to do any of that and fallen in love all over again.

When it was all said and done, Clark didn't want to see her leave. Especially on rocky terms. It felt like their last few months of med school all over again. Only this time, the pain was somehow even more excruciating. Eva was going back to a man who didn't deserve her rather than stay in Las Vegas and give the two of them a real chance.

Maybe it's time to risk it all and fight for the only woman you've ever really wanted...

Clark, suddenly growing hot with confusion, pushed away from the table. "Are we done here, Dr. Beal?"

"I think so. Dr. Gordon can catch you up on the rest of the patients' cases, none of which are as extreme as Mr. Cuttington's. And *I* can go home and get some rest."

"Sounds good," Clark told him before hopping up and headed toward the door.

"Wait, Dr. Malone?" Eva said.

He stopped in the doorway, refusing to turn around. "Yes?"

"Would you mind hanging back for a few minutes? I need to speak with you."

Feeling as though he might catch fire, Clark fanned himself with Mr. Cuttington's test results. "I'm actually late for a meeting. Why don't we reconvene inside the ER?"

Before she could respond, he charged out of the room and headed straight to Leo's office.

CHAPTER FIFTEEN

Month three

"ARE YOU SURE Clark's not gonna be here?" Eva asked Brandi for the fourth time.

"Yes, Eva. I'm positive. Tonight is for us girls only. No boys allowed."

Unconvinced, Eva followed her inside the Oasis. "Mmm-hmm. We'll see. I'm only asking because Clark does not want to see me. He's managed to remain professional at work, but underneath it all, I can tell he'd rather eat thumbtacks than be in my presence."

"What makes you think that?"

"Well, he's avoided me at every opportunity, and he's refused to speak to me privately. He hasn't returned my phone calls or responded to my texts. Honestly, I just don't think he's interested anymore, and he wasn't even before Kyle arrived. Maybe this fling was all he needed to get closure from our past. Once I'm gone, he'll probably go right back to playing the field."

"Ha! I highly doubt that. But just to ease your mind, I swear to you that Clark will not be here."

As the pair squeezed through the crowd in search of an empty table, Eva was reminded of the first day she'd hung out there with Brandi, Leo and Clark. That same tsunami of emotions swirled through her head. Only this time, she wasn't fretting over her and Clark's past. Instead she was drowning in the murky waters of their present. How in the hell had she and Clark managed to make such a mess of their situation once again?

Why are you asking yourself questions that you already know the answers to?

Both she and Clark had mishandled their fling from day one. She'd wanted more than just a casual hookup but refused to speak up after he'd laid the ground rules. And from what Eva had gathered, he saw her as nothing more than a woman on the rebound he could enjoy a commitment-free fling with, who wouldn't put any demands on him beyond great sex. The old Clark never would've settled for an emotionless hookup, knowing there was so much more between them. But these days he seemed content being a player with no attachments. Eva knew this way of life would never bring him true happiness. Nevertheless, she felt she had no choice but to accept his wishes, just as he'd accepted hers back in the day.

Reconnecting with Clark had been magical. There was no denying their organic bond and fiery chemistry. Despite never having said the words, he'd made her feel loved. Yet through it all, he'd refused to break their agreement and open up emotionally. So she'd continued to follow his lead and do the same.

Now here they were, ending on a bitter note the second time around.

Suddenly, Eva was overcome by the urge to leave. Go back to her apartment and break down in a hot, soothing bath. Or maybe even start packing so that the moment her assignment was over, she could jet back to Black Willow.

"Is this good?" Brandi asked, pointing to an empty table.

"This is fine."

Right after they sat down and placed their order, Brandi got straight to it. "So, what's the final verdict on you and Clark?"

"Bottom line? This was just a fling that was stamped with an expiration date from the very beginning. And now our time is almost up. He'll go his way and I'll go mine. Now can we please change the subject and officially kick off our girls' night?"

Brandi glanced down at Eva's left hand. "Yes. We can. But before we do, can I ask just one more question?"

"I'm listening," Eva said before shoving a

chicken nacho doused in cheese and salsa inside her mouth.

"What's the deal with you and your ex? I mean, I know he came here and proposed. Are you really gonna go back home and marry him?"

"I hadn't planned on it."

"But you're open to giving him another chance? To seeing where the relationship might go?"

"Honestly, no. I just haven't had a chance to tell Kyle that yet. I've tried calling, but I guess he's been so busy with work that he hasn't had a chance to call back. Maybe he's avoiding me because he knows what's coming. But we're done. And when I return to Black Willow, I'll just have to weather the storm of our breakup."

Brandi's eyes narrowed as she studied the bar's entrance. "Oh, *damn*."

"Oh, damn, what?"

Eva pivoted in her chair. Craning her neck, she noticed Leo dancing his way through the crowd.

"What is Leo doing here?"

"I have no idea. I did tell him we'd be here, but only because I didn't want him showing up with Clark. I made it very clear that he should stay away, and he and I would get together later."

"That's all right," Eva said, turning back around and taking a sip of her drink. "I don't mind Leo joining us. He's always a fun time. And I think it's cute how he can't seem to stay away from you—"

"Hello, ladies," a deep, all-too-familiar voice said behind her that didn't belong to Leo. "I didn't expect to see you two here. I wonder who set *this* up."

A knot of nausea bounced inside the pit of Eva's stomach.

Clark.

She sat stiffly in her seat, her hands already trembling with anxiety.

"What's up, my good people?" Leo boomed, plopping down in the chair next to Brandi's. "What are we drinking?"

"How about *I* start with the questions," Brandi retorted. "What are you doing here, Leo? Didn't I tell you that Eva and I made plans for just the two of us, and that we'd hang out later?"

"Yeah, you did. But my man Clark here mentioned that he wanted to grab a beer after work because we had such a long day. So I figured, *hey*, why not stop by our favorite spot? Where everybody knows our name? And they're always glad we came?"

"That's not exactly how it happened," Clark interjected, hovering over the chair next to Eva's as if waiting for an invitation to sit down. "You told me that—"

"Who cares about all the irrelevant little details?" Leo interrupted. "What matters most is that the gang's all here now! I see you two already have your drinks. Clark, I'll go grab us a couple of vodka martinis. Brandi, why don't you come and help me carry them back to the table?"

"You've got two hands. Why can't you go by your—"

Before she could finish, Leo grabbed her by the waist and pulled her away from the table.

And then there were two.

From the corner of her eye, Eva noticed Clark's fingers tapping the back of the chair next to hers.

"Do you mind if have a seat?" he finally asked.

"Not at all."

Her cool tone was a complete contradiction to the flaming nerves burning inside her throat.

"How's that old-fashioned?" he asked.

"It's good. Would you like a taste?"

Now why in the hell did you ask him that?

Eva squeezed her glass, mad that she'd already dropped her chilly facade. But then she glanced over at him and saw a slight smile on his face, highlighting that deep dimple in his left cheek.

Okay, maybe Clark's come in peace tonight.

"No, thanks. I'll wait for Leo to get back with my drink."

He glanced down at her left hand, then back up at her.

"Where's your ring?"

"What ring?"

"The ring that the senator proposed to you with when he came to town."

"It's…um…back at the apartment."

"So when is the wedding?"

"There isn't going to be a wedding."

"Really?" Clark slid his chair closer to Eva's. "From the looks of things when I saw you two together, it seemed as if you'd accepted his proposal."

"Well, looks can be deceiving. Because I didn't."

"So you shot him down? Told him no?"

Eva squirmed underneath Clark's intense gaze. "Put it this way… I didn't tell him yes."

Raising his head toward the ceiling, Clark blinked rapidly, as if his next question was buried within the copper tin tiles. "But you didn't actually tell him no either."

"Not yet. But I will," she snapped.

"Are you sure? Because I know how badly your parents want you to be with someone like him."

"My parents want me to be happy," Eva shot back.

"And being a part of Black Willow's high society, on a senator's arm, wouldn't make you happy? Because after all, you didn't turn down Kyle's proposal and send him home with that ring in his suitcase. Which would leave the door open for you two to get married," he said pointedly.

"What do you care, Clark? You've been pulling away from me emotionally over the past few weeks. Since all you seemed to want me for in the first place was sex, why are you so concerned now with who wants to marry me?"

"*Eva*. None of that is—"

"And we're back!" Leo proclaimed, interrupting the pair. He handed Clark a drink, then rejoined them at the table along with Brandi. "What'd we miss?"

"*Nothing,*" Eva and Clark declared in unison.

"I.e. a hell of a lot," Leo said drily.

The DJ turned down the music and hopped on the mic.

"Hello, hello, hello, my party people!" he crooned.

Eva took several sips of her drink, glad for the interruption. The heated exchange between her and Clark had brought on a mist of sweat. She grabbed a napkin and dabbed at her neck.

"You missed a spot," Clark said, running his fingertip along the edge of her throat.

Eva gazed at him. His expression was just as surprised as hers at his involuntary action. Their sexual chemistry was clearly still ever present and beyond palpable, despite their heated argument.

She pressed her thighs together as the sensation of his skin tickled her most sensitive spot.

Don't do this. Do not let this man get the best of you...

"Welcome to Benny B.'s Raging Eighties Dance Party!" the DJ continued. "I'll be playing some of the greatest hits of the decade while you good people tear up the dance floor. Now, drink up, eat up, tip these hardworking bartenders well and, most importantly, have a good time. Let's *go*!"

Janet Jackson's "The Pleasure Principle" blared through the speakers. The crowd roared, their bodies bumping into one another as they rushed the dance floor.

Without saying a word, Leo turned to Brandi and held out his hand.

"You know Janet is my all-time favorite," she said to Eva. "Do you mind?"

"No, of course not. Go on. Have fun."

That's what her mouth said. But Eva's mind buzzed with worry at the thought of Clark starting back up once they were alone again.

"So," he began the moment Leo and Brandi were out of earshot.

Here we go...

"Your time here in Las Vegas is coming to an end soon."

"Yep. It is."

"How do you feel about that?"

Eva knew what he was doing. Probing her. Baiting her. Trying to analyze her mindset. If she told him the truth, would her feelings simply feed into his ego? Make him feel as though he'd finally conquered his biggest challenge? She hated their back-and-forth battles. The tit-for-tat struggle for power. Their unwillingness to be the first to show vulnerability and reveal their true emotions.

"How do I feel about it?" Eva repeated. "Bittersweet." There. Just enough to chew on without putting it all on the line. "How do you feel about it?"

"The same. Bittersweet."

Touché.

Tonight, they were both playing a mental game of chess, not checkers.

Eva watched as Clark took a sip of his drink. Déjà vu teased her brain as she'd studied that mouth so many times before. The way his soft, full lips skimmed the edge of the glass. His long, strong, flexible fingers reaching down and pulling the toothpick from the rim. Sliding it between his lips. Sucking the olive and chewing it slowly. He knew she was watching. And he made sure to put on a show.

"How's your drink?" she asked.

"Good. Would you like to taste it?"

"Sure."

Rather than hand her the glass, Clark reached over and held it to her lips. She took a sip. When he pulled it away, vodka trickled down his index finger. He ran it along her bottom lip. She licked it right before the alcohol dribbled down her chin.

Oh, he's not playing fair...

Clark placed the glass down and pulled in a long breath of air. "Eva, can I be honest with you about something?"

"Of course." Her muscles tensed as she braced herself. Was he finally going to profess his feelings for her?

"I don't like all this tension between us. To put it bluntly, I've been miserable because of it. I don't want to fight with you anymore. Since your time left here is limited, let's just call a truce. End things on a high note. Enjoy the rest of your stay in Vegas, then commit to maintaining some semblance of a friendship once you return to Black Willow."

It wasn't quite what Eva had expected to hear. She wanted Clark to fight for her. To ask for more. To tell her that he was done with his serial dating ways and was ready to commit to her. But Eva knew Clark didn't have that in him. So she had no choice but to accept the limitations of what he was able to give her.

"I don't want to fight with you anymore either," she told him. "Honestly, I was ecstatic when you and I reestablished our friendship. And the intimate moments we've shared have been nothing short of amazing. We both agreed to remain open, have fun and enjoy each other's company. Which we did. But then we allowed our emotions to get the best of us. And that's when things got...*complicated*. For the part I played in that, I apologize."

Clark leaned in and placed a tender kiss on her lips. "Thank you for that. And for whatever part I played, I apologize, too."

Despite feeling devastated that this was likely their ending, Eva was glad to have finally healed their years-long rift and made memories that she would forever cherish.

"So, we're good?" she asked, holding out her hand.

"We're good."

He took Eva's hand and pulled her close, then slid his hand into her hair. She gasped, shocked that he was showing such a public display of affection. Pressing his mouth against hers, he slipped his tongue between her lips while gently massaging her scalp. The euphoric sensation had her contemplating sneaking him inside the bathroom to finish what he'd started.

"You wanna get out of here?" he whispered in her ear, his tongue lightly nuzzling her lobe.

"Absolutely."

No sooner than the response was out of her mouth, Eva felt Clark's phone vibrate against her thigh. Flashbacks of their first night at the Oasis, when he'd rushed out to meet up with another woman, deflated her swelling excitement.

She slowly moved away and drained her glass, anticipating him remembering he'd already made other plans.

Clark pulled the phone from his pocket. Eva's gaze couldn't help but to drift toward the screen. She held on to the edge of the table as he swiped open the home page. Would it be a text? A missed call? A message alert from one of his dating apps?

A list of notifications appeared. The latest one that had just come in was at the very top. A white box with the red letter "E" skirted the left side of the screen. To the right of it was a breaking news headline.

You are being ridiculous, Eva told herself, chomping down on a piece of ice in shame.

Clark put the phone away and stood, holding out his hand. "Shall we?"

"Yes."

They made their way toward the door, peering at the dance floor in search of Leo and Brandi. When the foursome made eye contact, Eva and Clark pointed at the exit then waved goodbye, prompting Brandi and Leo to wave back.

Eva felt as though she were starring in her very own movie as Clark whisked her straight to his car. While she may well be heading for heartbreak, Eva decided to simply enjoy the ride before the inevitable crash.

* * *

By the time Eva and Clark landed in his bed, there were no words left to be said. The pair lay together, taking their time while gently caressing each other. Eva soaked up the moment knowing they'd never get it back. Peering up at Clark, she saw him in a different light that glowed with a newfound appreciation. He was so special, and she'd always regret not seeing that years ago. But she knew now she had done too much damage to his trust for things to ever to work out between them.

Clark parted Eva's legs, then nestled his body between them. Holding her arms above her head, their fingers instinctively intertwining. Their lips met, their tongues danced, then went deeper.

Their naked bodies turned in unison. His erection pressed against her, slipping, sliding, teasing. She rolled her hips, throbbing as the tip circled her opening.

"Uh-uh," Clark grunted. "Not yet. I want to relish every moment of this."

The words melted her body underneath his touch. His spell. His prowess. Her moans vibrated against his neck. She bit down, wanting to savor the moment as well but growing impatient to the point of fatigue. He slid down the bed, his tongue trailing her body along the way, from her lips to her ears, her neck to her breasts.

He grazed her nipples with his teeth, causing her breathing to quicken.

"You've got to stop this," she pleaded. "I'm on the verge of exploding."

"I'd love to see it."

She arched her back, her nails skimming his scalp, her hands massaging his broad shoulders and smooth, bulging biceps. Having no mercy, he continued toward the edge of the bed. Eva closed her eyes, the sensation of his mouth covering every inch of her body as he devoured the sensitive skin on her stomach, her hips, in between her thighs.

Trembling with expectation, she spread her legs farther apart. He threw them over his shoulders. His face disappeared as he reached up and teased her nipples with his fingertips. She ground her hips to the rhythm of his tongue sliding up and down, in and out. When it stroked upward and caressed her nub, his fingers took its place, slowly gliding inside her.

Eva gripped the sides of his face, unable to hold back the guttural scream that released from deep within. She shivered uncontrollably as he gripped her hips, his mouth remaining firmly between her legs.

"I can't do this anymore," she groaned, locking her hands underneath his arms and pulling him up.

This time, he obliged. Their lips met again.

He pulled her toward him, finally slipping inside. She sighed into his mouth, surrendering her entire body to Clark. Pouring everything within her into that moment. Her arms clutched his back while her legs straddled his neck. She thrashed against him and when he went deeper, she pushed back harder, the pleasure escalating with every move.

Clark's thrusts slowly intensified. Eva clenched her muscles in response, relishing every inch of his length while licking his sweat from her lips. His head rose from her breasts. Their eyes met. Emotions poured from his gaze. She could feel the bliss. The desire. And sense the regret.

But behind the pleasure was a hint of sadness. She felt that, too. In the back of their minds lay the constant reminder that her departure was imminent. Time had become a thief of joy, transforming the thought of home into a notion of dread.

Clark's arms tightened around her. His embrace dissolved the angst that invaded the moment. He brought her to a peak as she closed her eyes, her body stiffening, then trembling. When he called out her name she released, biting into his neck as he exploded inside her, ending their night on the highest note yet.

CHAPTER SIXTEEN

Eva stirred slightly as sunlight burned her eyelids. She squinted, briefly forgetting where she was.

Still at Clark's place, in his bed...

Once her blurred vision cleared, she saw him sauntering toward her, fully dressed.

"Good morning, beautiful," he said, pressing his lips against hers.

She wrapped her fingers around his neck, contemplating tearing off his clothes. "Me, beautiful? In all my tousled-haired, smeared-makeup glory?"

"Yes, you, in all of that."

"Why are you already up and dressed instead of lying in bed next to me?"

"Mmm," Clark moaned. "As much as I'd love to be doing just that, I have a community service event to go to. My fraternity brothers and I are hosting a clothing drive at the Earl's House men's shelter."

"You know, I love a man who can help the less

fortunate in his free time, when he isn't on the clock saving lives."

"Excuse me, but did I just hear you say the L-word?"

"I don't know. Did you?"

"Yeah, I believe I did."

While waiting tensely to see where he was going with that, Eva's cell phone buzzed. Clark grabbed it off the nightstand.

"Uh-oh," he uttered drily. "Look who it is, FaceTiming you while you're laid up at your secret lover's house. Your mother."

Eva snatched the phone and quickly declined the video chat.

"What are you doing? You should've picked up. Told your mom I said hello and found out what she wanted. You never know. Something could be wrong."

"Trust me, nothing is wrong. She's probably calling to harass me about putting the wedding plans back in motion. And the last thing I need her to see is me sprawled out naked in some man's bed."

The moment the words were out of her mouth, Eva regretted them. Especially when she felt the warmth drain from Clark's body. He stood rigidly, shoving his keys inside his pocket.

"Wait," she uttered. "I didn't mean it like that. I already told you I did not accept Kyle's proposal."

"But you didn't tell him no either, did you?"

"Come on, Clark. I was in shock! The last thing I expected was for Kyle to pop up in Las Vegas and ask me to marry him."

His mouth compressed. "When it comes down to it, what would your parents prefer? For you to marry Kyle, or to continue sleeping with me?"

Eva couldn't lie to him, so she remained silent.

"Exactly," Clark said coolly. "Still living for everybody except yourself."

Eva hopped out of bed and threw on her clothes, acting as if she hadn't heard him. But she had, loud and clear. She could sense his mind flipping through their past, recalling how determined she'd been in school to please her parents and thinking they were the reason she didn't move forward with him. Nothing she said was going to convince him he was wrong about her.

Clark's words from last night popped into her mind.

Since your time here is limited, let's just call a truce. Enjoy the rest of your stay in Las Vegas, then commit to maintaining some semblance of a friendship once you return to Black Willow.

Eva wanted nothing more than to do just that. But somehow, she and Clark had managed to hit an emotional roadblock at every turn. And she knew why. Their walls of protection were still standing tall. Neither of them had been willing to let their guard down and reveal their whole selves. The taste of pain they'd both endured during this tumultuous fling was enough to deter any admission that could make them vulnerable. Fear overrode honesty. They were both running hot, reluctant to test the other's flame.

Clark's lack of trust in her was still apparent, and it still stung. It felt as if he'd always have an issue with her parents and Kyle. Eva was almost ready to give up on him altogether considering he didn't seem to believe in them as a couple. Walking away with what was left of her heart intact felt like the right thing to do, rather than trying to repeatedly make the impossible happen.

But when she looked up at him and saw his somber expression, and the sadness in his eyes, Eva knew she couldn't leave things this way.

"Do you have time to grab coffee before your event?" she asked, hoping the olive branch would somehow smooth things over.

Barely glancing at his watch, Clark replied, "No, I'm actually running late. I was supposed to be at the shelter over thirty minutes ago. But you were sleeping so well that I didn't want to wake you."

His thoughtfulness made her chest pull tight as her mind immediately went to Kyle. He would've woken her up two hours early if it meant being on time for an event.

"How about getting together later?" she pressed. "Maybe for lunch, or an early dinner?"

"Lunch won't work because we're serving food at the shelter from noon to three. I'll get back to you on dinner. The rest of my day is still up in the air."

In other words, he's really not trying that hard to see me despite what he said about making the most of the rest of my time here.

The ride back to Eva's building was silent for the most part, except for the R&B music playing in the background. As soon as Clark pulled into the driveway Eva swung open the door.

"Thanks," she said, her heart practically pounding out of her chest with sadness and loss. "I guess I'll um…see you at the hospital."

"Yep. See you there."

After Clark sped off, Eva stared up at her building's cold mirrored windows. The last thing she wanted to do was sit inside her apartment alone with her thoughts. Instead, she headed over to the coffee shop and treated herself to a strawberry Frappuccino. The outdoor patio was empty, so she took a seat in the sun, catching the last bits of morning rays before they transformed into beaming afternoon scorchers.

She looked out at the palm leaves swaying from the majestic treetops. The morning smog had lifted, leaving a clear view of the Spring Mountains' spectacular peaks in the distance.

I'm going to miss this, she thought as images

of Black Willow's flat land and bulky white oaks sprang to mind.

The moment was disrupted by an incoming FaceTime call. Without looking, Eva already knew who it was. A rumble of dread lurched through her stomach as she tapped the accept button. She put on a forced smile when her mother's face appeared, all the while thinking, *If she starts going in about Kyle and the wedding, I'm hanging up.*

Times like this made her regret being born with the parent-pleasing gene. She appreciated how her father's work as a family practitioner had motivated her to become a doctor. But she should've drawn the line when her bougie mother, who'd wanted a better life for her only child than the one she'd had, had continued on that path a little too rigidly.

"Wilson!" her mother called out. "It's Eva. Come and say hello!"

"I'm on my way!"

Her mother ran a French-manicured hand along the edges of her silverish gray pixie cut, clearly staring at her own image rather than Eva.

"Hello, Mom."

"Hello, my love," she replied, her matte red lips blowing air kisses at the screen. "How do you think our new house is looking? Did Valerie and I do a fabulous job with the decorating or what?"

"Yes, you two did." Eva pulled the screen closer as her mother scanned the living room.

Her parents had moved into the ranch style home a few months ago after her mother had insisted on selling the trilevel house they'd owned for almost thirty years, declaring she could no longer climb staircases that resembled Mount Everest.

"Do you like all of the new pieces?" her mother continued, pointing toward acrylic accent tables, a tufted beige sofa and a white sheepskin rug.

"Yes, Mother, everything is beautiful. Where's Dad? I thought he was coming out."

"I can hear him bopping around here somewhere. I'll go to him since he refuses to come to us."

The minute her mother stepped inside their sleek white kitchen, her father appeared. "There's my girl!" he cried.

"Hey, Dad! It's so good to see your face. How are you doing?"

"Great, other than trying to keep your mother from spending all my money. How's it going out there in the Wild, Wild West?"

"Really well. I'm enjoying the challenging work, the excitement of the city, the amazing people—"

"And when is this assignment of yours going to be over again?" her mother interrupted.

Eva's father wrapped his arm around her. "The

same time it's always been scheduled to end, Iris. At the end of the month. Now, let's not get started on this again."

"Who's getting started, Wilson? I'm just trying to have a conversation with our daughter."

He gave her chin an affectionate squeeze. Eva smiled softly as she watched them stare lovingly at each other. Her father may be graying a bit at the temples, and her mother crinkling around the eyes. But their passion for each other never seemed to fade, even after all these years.

This is what I want. What I should be working toward...

"I'm glad to hear things are going well, honey," her father said. "I knew that working in a big-city ER would be an invaluable experience for you."

"Thanks, Dad. It really has been."

Her mother pulled the phone in her direction. "I'm glad, too, hon. It just seems like you've been gone forever. I'm ready for my daughter to come back home. We all are. Black Willow is where you belong. You've given enough of yourself to Las Vegas. And let's be honest. That place isn't really *you*, now, is it?"

"What do you mean by that?"

"What I mean is, you're a class act, Eva. An intelligent, dignified woman who was raised to be an outstanding leader within the Black Willow community. Your talents are far better served right here at home. Not across the country in some desert party city."

"You've been talking to Kyle again, haven't you?"

A twist of her mother's lips was all it took for Eva to guess the answer. *Yes.*

"You know, Mom, not only has Las Vegas made me a better doctor, but it's made me a better person. I was just telling a wonderful new friend I made here how I've opened up to so many things, done some exploratory work on myself, come to terms with what I want out of life. And to be honest, my aspirations are beginning to shift."

Her mother turned to her father, mumbling, "What exactly is she trying to tell us?"

"I'm not one hundred percent sure. But whatever it is, I like the sound of it."

"I'll tell you what, honey," her mother continued. "When you come home, you can show all the townspeople how much you've grown, then *really* put the icing on the cake by putting your wedding back on the calendar. Let them know that you and Kyle are back together and better than ever."

"But Kyle and I are not back together. And why should we be? I couldn't imagine being in love with someone, then dumping them over the pressures of my career. Dad, did you ever consider leaving Mom when things got tough during medical school? Or while you were struggling to open your own practice?"

"No. Not for a second."

"I rest my case."

Her mother handed the phone to her father with a pout, then poured two glasses of mimosas. "I never could get through to that child…"

Eva picked at the paint chipping along the edge of her wrought iron chair, thinking back on her evening with Clark, then remembering his reaction when her mother called that morning. She shouldn't have held off on sharing with her parents how Clark had been the highlight of her trip.

"You know," Eva began, "I actually reconnected with an old friend during my stay here."

"Really?" her mother asked. "Who?"

"Clark Malone."

A warm breeze of satisfaction blew over her at the sound of his name. Eva knew she was too damn old to be so concerned with what her parents thought.

Her mother stared into space while tapping her fingernail against the counter. "Clark Malone, Clark Malone…" she uttered, as if repeating his name would help jog her memory. "That doesn't ring a bell. Wilson, do you remember a Clark Malone?"

"Didn't you two attend medical school together?" he asked.

"Yes, we did."

"Yeah, I remember him. I always liked that kid. If I can recall correctly, you two were pretty good friends, but then you lost touch. What is he up to these days?"

"He's an ER doctor at Fremont General."

"Oh, is he?" her father asked, his head nodding with approval.

Her mother grabbed the phone and shoved it close to her face. "Hold on, Eva. Is that what this trip was really about? You running off to Las Vegas to get together with someone from your past?"

"No, Mom, not at all. I had no idea Clark was even living in Vegas, let alone working at the hospital. But having him here to show me the ropes and adjust to the city has been great. Really great."

With a dismissive wave of her hand, her mother replied, "Well I'm glad you've had a colleague there to assist you. But now that this assignment is coming to an end, it's time to start focusing on your return to Black Willow and how you're going to get back with—"

"Clark isn't just some colleague," Eva interrupted defiantly. "He is a friend. A very close friend…" As her voice trailed off, Eva realized that she'd had enough for one day. "You know, I'm sitting out in this hot sun, and I've got some things I need to take care of back at the apartment. So I'm gonna go."

"Okay," her mother responded. "But before you do, please just let me say this."

Here it was. The moment Eva had been dreading, when her mother would endorse Kyle as if their relationship was yet another campaign and he was running to win her back.

"Iris," her father said, "our daughter has things to do. Why don't we hang up before she gets sunburned?"

"I'll just be a minute. Eva, listen to me, sweetheart. Kyle flew all the way out to Las Vegas, right after he won the election no less, to apologize and propose again with that gorgeous new ring. I know he hurt you, but he was under so much pressure during that intense campaign. Please, at least consider giving him another chance. He's a good man, and I don't want you to miss out on a wonderful life—"

"Eva," her father interjected, "your mother and I want you to do whatever makes you happy. If that means giving Kyle another chance, fine. If it doesn't, that's fine, too. In the meantime, enjoy the rest of your days in Las Vegas, and we will talk to you soon."

Eva blew him a kiss, grateful for his understanding.

"Any parting words, Iris?" he asked her mother.

"Now you already know the answer to that. Eva, I want nothing more than for you to be happy. And I'm sorry if I'm being a little pushy. But as your mother, I cannot help but think I know what's best for you. However, like your father said, if marrying Kyle isn't in your future, then I'll just have to accept that. We love you, miss you, and can't wait for you to come home."

"Thank you. I love you, too. Oh, and before I forget, Clark told me to tell you both hello."

"Who?" her mother chirped.

Right before her father said, "Please tell Dr. Malone we said hello, and congratulations on all his success."

"I will. Talk soon."

Eva disconnected the video chat and immediately composed a text to Clark.

Just spoke with my parents. Told them you said hello. They said hello back, and congratulations on all your success.

While it was clear that things weren't going to work out between them, Eva couldn't shake the need to prove to Clark that he wasn't some taboo secret she was keeping from her parents.

Within seconds, he responded.

Please thank them for me. That means a lot. More than you know.

The reply gave her a slight glimmer of hope that maybe, just maybe, things between them could still be salvaged.

CHAPTER SEVENTEEN

CLARK SETTLED IN at a table inside the physician's lounge with his iced green tea and spinach breakfast wrap in hand. The moment he pulled out his cell phone and began scrolling the apps, Eva came walking through the door.

Remorse throbbed inside his chest as he watched her approach the coffee station. Eva's time at Fremont General was coming to an end. While her stay had endured its fair share of ups and downs, he hated how when it came to them, she'd be leaving on a low note. How had they managed to fumble their friendship once again? For his part, Clark's intention of keeping things casual and holding back his feelings had blown up in his face. And now he had no clue where they stood.

He and Eva hadn't spoken outside of work since their last text message exchange, when she'd shared her parents' greeting. The fact that she'd mentioned him to them did give some semblance of him hope. And now, as he watched her chatting with a group of doctors, he wondered if she'd notice him sitting there, and come join him if he asked.

Even in her white coat and scrubs, Eva appeared beautiful and graceful. Everyone inside the lounge greeted her warmly, asking how she'd enjoyed her time at the hospital and when her assignment would end.

"Soon," Clark heard her tell one of the physicians. "Very soon…"

Hearing that response sent a mouthful of tea down the wrong pipe. Clark pounded his chest and cleared his throat, struggling to prevent a fit of coughs. The commotion caught the attention of several physicians, Eva included.

Clark's skin burned with embarrassment as he nodded, letting them all know he was okay. When he and Eva locked eyes, she gave a small wave. Her tentative smile prompted him to gesture the empty chair next to him. As she sauntered over, the remorse swirling inside his chest settled into a wave of excitement.

"Hey, good morning," he said.

"Good morning. How are you?"

If her breathy tone was any indication of how she was feeling, Eva was just as nervous as he was.

"Hanging in there. You know…"

"Yeah, I do know." Eva fiddled with the lid on her cup, her head tilting to one side. "I'm not used to seeing you here in the mornings. You're usually hanging out in the cafeteria or the ER conference room."

"I know. I wanted to do a little cleanup on my phone, and I'm doing it in here because the cafeteria is so noisy and the conference room is in use." Clark left out the part where he was hoping to run into Eva since she usually stopped by the lounge most mornings.

Eva peered down at his phone screen. "What's going on with your cell? Are you running out of memory? Or is it freezing up?"

"No, nothing like that. Just getting rid of the stuff that no longer serves me."

As Eva looked on, Clark's first instinct was to hide the phone. But considering she was the main reason for the cleanup, he didn't bother.

"Wait a minute," she said, nudging his arm. "Did I just see you delete the Two of Hearts dating app?"

"Yes, you did," he confirmed as he continued clicking the *X* hovering over several other apps.

"Oh, and Swipe Right Tonight and Struck by Cupid's Arrow are getting the axe, too?

"Yep. Gone."

"So what brought on this?"

Clark set his cell to the side and looked her in the eye. "Honestly? They weren't doing me any good. I wasn't getting anything out of juggling a bunch of different women, then running away when things got serious. That was just my way of masking the underlying issues I hadn't faced regarding my past. The heartbreaks that I never dealt with. Then when you showed up here in Vegas, and we got involved again, I was forced to confront that pain. Last time I ran around it. This time I'm going through it. Dealing with it head-on until I heal. I can't do that if I'm focusing on a bunch of frivolous, casual hookups."

Clark blew a long exhale after finally releasing that heavy burden. He'd surprised himself after sharing all that with Eva. But it was the truth, and she deserved to hear it before she left. Plus, if he was planning on doing things differently in the future, expressing how he felt without fear was a good place to start.

"Wow," Eva uttered, watching him intently. "I, um… I didn't expect you to say that. Thank you for being so open with me. That's actually wonderful to hear, Clark. And no matter what comes of us, I do care about you a great deal. I want you to be happy. But that won't happen until you heal. So hearing you say you're working toward that is really amazing. You'll be a better man for it."

"Thanks, Eva. That's my hope."

After taking a long sip of coffee, she asked, "So, where do things stand with us?"

"Well, your assignment ends in a couple of weeks. And at this point, I have nothing to lose.

So I feel perfectly at peace telling you that I love you, Eva. And I wish you weren't leaving. I hate the idea of you going back to Black Willow and even considering marrying Kyle. I know I messed up by letting fear get in the way and diminishing our relationship to a casual hookup. We could've spent this time together working toward building something real. If I could go back and do things differently, I would. But I can't. So I'm forced to deal with my mistakes and hope that we can still salvage our friendship."

Falling against the back of her chair, Eva gazed at Clark through wide eyes. "I—I don't even know what to say to that. You love me?"

"I do. Very much. But I also know that you have some unfinished business back in Iowa, and I don't wanna get in the way of that. You need to be clear on what you want. If that's me, then you have got to tell Kyle that it's over for good and give him that ring back." Clark reached over and slid her hand in his. "I really want to try to make something of us, Eva. And I don't care if there's fifteen hundred miles between us. That's just a plane ride away."

Eva sat straight up, locking her fingers with Clark's. "You know what? I—"

The beep of the hospital intercom filled the lounge, interrupting her mid-sentence.

"Dr. Malone, please report to the emergency room. Dr. Malone to the emergency room."

"Dammit," Clark groaned, glancing at his watch. "I had thirty minutes left until my day was scheduled to begin. Listen, let's continue this conversation right after I check into the ER and find out what's going on."

She sighed in frustration as he shot out the door. She'd wanted to say, *I love you, too, Clark.*

But now she'd have to wait.

An hour later, Eva's entire body was buzzing with joy as she exited the physicians' on-call room. She shouldn't have been this happy after telling Kyle that they were done considering the news had upset him. But in the back of her mind, all Eva could think about was the fact that Clark had just professed his love for her, even if he didn't know her feelings yet. There wasn't enough begging in the world Kyle could have done, which he'd certainly tried, to make her go back to him. She was moving on to better things.

After hanging up from him, Eva had called her parents to let them know that she had officially broken things off with Kyle for good. Her mother immediately began to unravel. But her father stopped the meltdown before it could really start, preventing her from ticking off all the reasons why Eva was making a mistake. Eva quickly interjected during the moment of silence, letting them both know how unhappy she'd been with Kyle, and that something more than just a friendship had sparked between her and Clark since she'd arrived in Las Vegas.

"Wait, what is that supposed to mean?" her mother had shrieked into the phone.

Once again, Eva's father came to her rescue, silencing her mother as Eva explained all the wonderful traits Clark brought to the table. "Not only that, but we're genuinely in love," she told her parents.

After a long silence, her mom asked, "Are you happy?" to which Eva replied, "Very."

Another extended pause ensued before her mother finally said, "Well, that's all that matters."

Eva checked her cell to see if Clark had reached out, then headed straight to the ER to find him. She rushed through the trauma units, operating rooms and observation areas. He was nowhere to be found. He wasn't inside the conference room, and neither Brandi nor Leo had seen him.

Just as Eva grabbed her phone to text him, it rang.

She eyed the screen, hoping it was Clark. Eva came to a grinding halt when Susan Piper's name appeared, the hospital administrator. That was odd considering she hadn't heard from Susan since the day she began her temporary assignment.

"Good morning, Dr. Gordon speaking."

"Good morning, Dr. Gordon. Susan Piper here. Do you have a free moment to stop by my office? I need to speak with you about something. It's urgent."

Eva's stomach dropped to her knees. "I do. I'll head there right now."

"Great. See you shortly."

What could be so wrong that I'm being called to the administrator's office?

After arriving on the third floor, Eva shuffled down the hallway, her teeth clenching to the rhythm of her clicking heels. One knock on the door and Susan called out, "Come in!"

Eva opened it slowly, sticking her head in first before entering.

"Please have a seat, Dr. Gordon."

I'm being let go early. She's going to send me back to Black Willow today, before I can even digest what just happened with Clark.

"Dr. Gordon, I just received word that Dr. Abrams will be leaving the hospital. His wife has accepted a position as the Caribbean Tourism Organization's new human resources director. So they'll be moving to Barbados. Soon."

Is this what I think it is? Eva asked herself, growing light-headed with anticipation as she stared across the desk.

"You have done an exceptional job here at Fremont General, Dr. Gordon. And I have received nothing but glowing feedback on your performance. Primarily from your former medical school classmate, Dr. Malone."

Wreathing her hands together, Eva rocked back in her chair, taking in the moment as it slowly sank in. "That is so nice to hear, Susan. Thank you."

"No, thank *you*. For all that you've done. And with that being said, we would like to offer you a permanent position here in the ER."

"Really?" Eva breathed, clutching her chest.

"Absolutely. I know it's a lot to think about. Las Vegas is a long way from Iowa. Your family is there, your friends. And I'm sure the staff at the Black Willow Medical Clinic would hate to see you go. But you seem to be enjoying your time here, and you've adjusted to our bustling emergency room beautifully. So, just think about it. Dr. Abrams isn't leaving for another few weeks, and I haven't even begun putting together a package for you. I just wanted to let you know what was happening so that you could consider it."

"You know what, Susan? Actually, it isn't a lot to think about. I haven't just enjoyed my time here at Fremont General, I've loved it. The people I've met, the things I've learned, the challenges I've faced. I came to Las Vegas looking for an escape and ended up finding a home. So I don't need time to think about it. I accept the offer."

"Wonderful!" Susan said, pressing her hands together. "I expect to have your package together within the next couple of days. Of course the salary will be competitive, and negotiable. But we'll work all that out. Until then, welcome aboard!"

"Thank you so much," Eva said, barely able to contain herself as she stood. "I look forward to the next steps."

"As do I. Thank you, Dr. Gordon."

Eva shot out of Susan's office and ran toward the elevator, texting Clark along the way. When she reached the first floor and rounded the corner, he appeared, almost knocking her to the floor.

"Sorry!" he exclaimed, grabbing her arms and lifting her up.

"I have been looking all over for you!" Eva exclaimed. "You will not *believe* all the new developments I have to share with you."

"Really? New developments since I last saw you about an hour ago?"

"Yes! Now let's go find someplace quiet so we can talk."

"Follow me."

Clark led Eva inside an empty consultation room. They sat close to each another on the burgundy tweed love seat, the energy between them vibrating at a feverish pitch.

"I must tell you—" Eva began before Clark interrupted her.

"Wait, before you start, I realized there were a few things I forgot to mention earlier when we spoke. Do you mind if I go first?"

"No, of course not," Eva lied, her knees bouncing impatiently as she was dying to share her news. Both the job offer and, more importantly, how much she loved him.

Clark took her hands in his. "I owe you the real explanation as to why I first suggested we only kept things casual between us. It had a lot to do with how you'd turned me down during med school. That rejection made me feel as if I wasn't good enough for you. And when I think about the man you were going to marry, I realize that I'm nothing like him. I'm not some stuffy politician from your hometown. The whole Black Willow pedigree means a lot to your parents, and I know how much their opinion means to you. So I figured you'd be more concerned with making them happy than making me happy."

Tears began trickling from Eva's eyes before words could escape her lips. As she opened her mouth to speak, Clark silenced her once again.

"Please, before you respond, just let me say that what we have is special. This is a once-in-a-lifetime kind of love. The kind of love that you deserve. From what you've told me, Kyle is not even close to being good enough for you. You'd be doing yourself a disservice giving him another chance. And I'm not just saying that because I want to be with you. I'm saying that because it's true. You're a good woman, Eva. You deserve the world. And I want to be the man to give it to you."

"Thank you, Clark. You deserve the same. And I *am* the woman who can give it to you. Because I love you, too. I was so confused when you suggested we keep things casual. But you were adamant, and I knew you had your reasons, so I just went along with it. That wasn't necessarily a bad thing, either. Because it gave me a chance to realize that you're the one for me. You always have been. Kyle isn't half the man that you are, and I can assure you that I will never go back to him. As a matter of fact, I just spoke to him and told him that."

"You did? When?"

"Right before I ran into you. So he is completely out of the picture. As for my parents, I spoke with them as well, letting them know that Kyle and I are done and there will definitely be no wedding."

"Did your mother faint?"

"Almost. But she eventually rebounded. Then when I told her and my father about us—"

"Hold on," Clark said, grabbing his head. "Now I think *I* might faint. You told your parents about us?"

"Yes, I did."

"What did they say?"

"Well, my father was fine with it. As for my mother, it took her a minute to come around. But eventually, she did. I convinced them both that you're an amazing man. And they reiterated that they just want me to be happy."

"I'm going to see to it that you are," Clark murmured, leaning in for a kiss.

Pressing her hands against his chest, Eva stopped him. "Wait. I have one more thing to share with you."

"Okay, let's hear it."

"I was just offered a permanent position here at Fremont General."

He leaped from the couch and pulled Eva to her feet. "What? *And?* Did you accept it?"

"I sure did."

Clark wrapped her up in a tight embrace, lifting her off the floor. "That is fantastic, Eva! You should've told me that the minute that door closed!"

"How could I after you insisted on talking first?"

"You make a good point." Clark paused, slowly lowering Eva. "You do know that everybody back in Black Willow will be devastated by this news, don't you?"

"I don't know about *devastated*. But I do think they'll be sad to see me go, for sure. However, just like my parents, they'd want me to do whatever makes me happy. So if that means moving to Vegas to take on this exciting new opportunity and be with the love of my life, then I'm sure I'll have their blessing."

"Mmm, the love of your life. I like the sound of that." Clark paused, his eyes drifting from Eva down to the pale gray carpeting. "Listen, I'm all for you moving to Las Vegas permanently, taking the job here at the hospital and us being together. But if we're really gonna do this, and I mean do it the right way, then I'm going to have to lay some ground rules."

Her body went limp within his embrace. "Here we go with these damn ground rules again. What is it going to be this time?"

"Well, obviously you'll no longer be my hookup buddy. But I don't want you to be my girlfriend, either."

"So what exactly am I going to be?"

"This time around, I want you to be my wife."

The air suddenly left the room. Eva stood there, frozen, her vision blurring as Clark got down on one knee. He took her left hand in his and kissed her ring finger.

"Now I know I'm not doing this the right way. This should've been planned out, our families and friends should be here, and I should have a stunning diamond ring to slip on your finger. But I'm hoping that my love for you will override all of that. At least for the time being. Eva Gordon, will you marry me?"

"Yes. Yes!" she squealed happily, pulling him up and jumping into his arms.

"Finally," he murmured in between kisses, "I got my girl back."

"Yes, you did. Thank you for being so patient with me, Clark. And for understanding that I needed time for my head and heart to align. I cannot wait to begin this new adventure with you. I love you, Clark Malone."

"I love you, too, Eva Gordon."

EPILOGUE

Six months later

EVA RELAXED HER head against the pillow and took a deep breath. "This feels so weird, being on the other side of things."

"I know it does," Clark agreed. "But this side of things looks good on you."

She looked up from the hospital bed at him and smiled, loving his newfound glow.

"Well," Dr. Hall said, turning their attention back to the monitor. "It looks like you're about thirteen weeks along, and according to the ultrasound, you're having a baby girl."

Tears of joy sprang from Eva's eyes as Clark leaned down and embraced her.

"Exactly what I wanted," he said huskily.

Eva chuckled, caressing his face before saying, "Stop lying. You know you wanted a boy!"

"That is *not* true. I'm happy either way. But this just means we'll have to keep trying…"

"For now, why don't we just focus on the bundle of joy we've got coming?" she suggested while focusing on the tiny gray image on the screen.

Life in Las Vegas had been a whirlwind ever since Eva had accepted the full-time position at Fremont General. After saying her goodbyes and selling her loft back in Black Willow, she'd packed up her things and moved into Clark's townhome. Then they'd found out about the baby, which had prompted them to host an intimate wedding ceremony for family and close friends at the Wynn. It was the first time they'd seen each other's parents since medical school. Eva was so pleased when hers welcomed Clark into the family with open arms. Her mother had become so ecstatic about the union and pregnancy that it was as if Kyle never existed. As for Clark's parents, they'd always been kind and accepting of Eva. It was as if no time had passed between them.

"Have you two thought of any baby names yet?" Dr. Hall asked.

"Of course I have," Eva said. "I love Simone, Nina, Devon, Eden…there are so many that I'm thinking of."

"What about you, Dr. Malone?"

"Honestly, I'm fine with whatever my wife chooses."

"Really? So you're not going to throw any names into the ring?"

"Doctor," Clark said, "I'm so happy to have this woman back in my life that she can pretty much do whatever she wants."

"Aww," Eva and Dr. Hall sighed in unison.

Dr. Hall pointed at Eva and said, "He's a keeper."

"Trust me, I know. Which is why I'm never letting him go."

The tears that had pooled along the rims of Eva's eyes slowly trickled down her cheeks. She still had trouble grasping how drastically things had changed within less than a year. From arriving in Las Vegas with a broken heart to falling in love with Clark, their second-chance romance was one for the books.

"Can you believe this?" he whispered, resting his hand against her belly. "That we're married, and pregnant, and getting to spend the rest of our lives together?"

"No, I cannot. It feels like a dream. There was a time when I never thought I'd find contentment. But this…this is far more than I could've ever hoped for. This is the ultimate happily-ever-after."

* * * * *